I0666351

VIRGIN ARMY BOY
Deflowered

First Edition

Published by The Nazca Plains Corporation
Las Vegas, Nevada
2009

ISBN: 978-1-935509-15-8

Published by

The Nazca Plains Corporation ®
4640 Paradise Rd, Suite 141
Las Vegas NV 89109-8000

PUBLISHER'S NOTE
Virgin Army Boy Deflowered is a work of fiction created wholly by *Bret Yerlac's* imagination. All characters are fictional and any resemblance to any persons living or deceased is purely by accident. No portion of this book reflects any real person or events.

Cover Photos, Vish Studio and Les Byerley
Art Director, Blake Stephens

DEDICATION

To The Memory Of

George Jennings and Alex Petroff
for their valued friendship,
for being the kind of people who
brought love into my home,
and made my life a joy
for many years.

VIRGIN ARMY BOY
Deflowered

First Edition

Bret Yerlac

CHAPTER ONE

Not really knowing what he wanted to do with his life, still only 20 years old, young Michael Hunt volunteered for the draft in the summer of 1960, soon after graduating with an AA degree from Junior College. By August he was at Fort Ord, CA completing his US Army basic training, then on to Fort Lewis, WA for another six weeks of Advance Infantry Training with an Infantry Division. It never seemed to stop raining during those six weeks of AIT in the state of Washington. For a native Californian, use to sunshine and warm weather, those weeks of playing war games in either the cold wet snow or what seemed like a constant downpour of rain proved gruelingly rough and depressing. With a bit of luck, a month after the AIT was completed, he was able to get himself reassigned from Company D, an Infantry Combat Unit, to Headquarters Company and assigned to work in the Personnel Department because of his education and office skills. Finally he was out of the rain and horrible harsh weather of the state of Washington and working inside out of the elements.

Private Hunt soon became Mike to the few guys he had befriended either in the personnel department or in headquarters company, and PFC Hunt or just Hunt to others. Mike was quite the looker, actually handsomely stunning to some and pretty by others. He had light blond hair, big light gray/blue eyes, high cheekbones, and a flawless creamy complexion. He stood at 5'11 with a narrow waist, wider hips and beautiful firm bubbled buns, the kind straight guys feast their eyes on and drool. If you were to see him in the shower with his back turned toward you, you would think he had the slim body of a young maiden with beautiful legs and an hourglass figure with an ass to die for and made for fucking. The areolas surrounding his large nipples were pink and nearly half dollar size. His smile displayed a perfect set of straight white ivories surrounded by puffy pink moist lips. He had little or no hair on his body or face, except for a patch of blond in each armpit and over his privates. He didn't have to shave but once or twice a week, and it was mostly to get rid of blond peach fuzz. He was uncircumcised with a perfectly shaped pinkish five inch flaccid cock set over a set of small hairless balls. He wasn't the least bit masculine in appearance or mannerisms. He had always been teased by the boys in high school, calling him 'My Cunt' sometimes, rather than Mike Hunt. This didn't set well with him, but he learned to tolerate the verbal innuendos along with guys occasionally running there hands over his soft skin as they played grab ass with him nude in the showers and locker room.

This didn't improve any in college and even got worse in the military's large communal showers. Guys eyed him with questioning eyes, especially the blacks that seem to have a reputation for liking blond white women. The blacks were attracted to him as a magnet is drawn to metal, feasting their eyes on him, making an effort to be in the showers at the same time as Michael. They would flaunt their huge endowments at Michael trying to get him turned on, assuming he had to be gay because he did have a few effeminate mannerisms and he certainly looked fantastic - the blond hair, the soft flawless skin, and especially those two fantastic bubble buns, the right one displaying a strawberry birthmark that stood out like an invitation that seemed to beckon 'Touch Me', 'Touch Me!' Frequently the bold ones did put on a show, sending Michael scurrying from the showers!

To avoid these embarrassing situations, Mike started waiting until well after midnight to take his shower when the huge tiled stall was empty. Using this tactic, he successfully avoided their shenanigans, at least in the showers. However, when he went out at night to the PX for a few beers and a bit of camaraderie, these same guys seemed to always be nearby.

They would buy him beer trying to get him loosened up so he would let down his guard so they could make a move on him. A couple of times one would almost get him cornered if he was walking alone back to the barracks, but managed to escape without getting molested.

You see, Michael had come from a very strict Southern Baptist family that had instilled in him at a very early age the preaching of the good book and the wrongs of homosexuality. Therefore, in reality, Mike was still a virgin at 20, except for pulling his own pud since he entered adolescence. He experienced wet dreams regularly, waking up with sticky boxers. He knew he wasn't attracted to women at all and had strong feelings for men, but had never allowed himself to partake in any experimenting with that forbidden sin of the flesh because of the strict religious beliefs he was taught as a Southern Baptist. Yes, Michael had a lot of religious baggage he carried around on his shoulders daily that became a burden to his social development – forbidden desires on the one side and religious taboos on the other. He was a nervous wreck by the time he graduated from Junior College, and here he was still a virgin with forbidden cravings constantly surfacing and making his life miserable.

So, Michael figured the solution to all his frustrations was to volunteer for the draft and spend the 18 months in the military getting his life in order. He came to the conclusion this would be the cure all to be rid of all the sinful desires that constantly haunted him, they would instantly disappear, because the military environment would make a real man of him. For a short time his plan was successful. He stayed busy and stayed away from situations where he might be tempted to partake in any kind of sexual activity. But soon he started having dreams, dreams where he was always involved with another man making love. Now that he was in an all male environment, constantly surrounded by men, his frustration and desires increased and became even worse. Keeping himself busy and isolated wasn't working anymore. Little by little his defenses tumbled and Michael started socializing and becoming part of the daily events in and about the barracks and immediate area.

Mike liked to gamble and learned to play poker quite well while attending college, though that too was taboo, as was dancing for any Southern Baptists. Never-the-less, now that he was in the service, it seemed that every payday a group of the guys would get together and a game of poker would get started. He became involved and would always do well, or at least break even. He became involved in many events around the base, even went into Tacoma and Seattle occasionally on weekends.

One payday he entered into a game of shooting dice with a bunch of the guys. He did quite well early on, considering he was a real greenhorn novice at the game. Most of the guys playing were black, as rolling dice was their specialty and they had mastered tossing those suckers very well indeed. They were also experienced at coning any unsuspecting neophyte, and Mike became their new mark. Being a real beginner they virtually fleeced PFC Mike Hunt of all his monthly pay, then only $59 as a private first class.

As Mike rose to his feet to leave the huddle of players, now flat broke, he headed for the stairwell leading to the second floor to go to his cubicle. Staff Sergeant Axel Wood stopped him and walked him aside to talk. The sergeant was one of Mike's coworkers in the personnel department. He had been watching the game from the sidelines. He proceeded to tell Mike of a sure fire strategy that would certainly make it possible for him to win some of his pay back from the winners. He encouraged Mike and virtually talked him back into the game using the three ten dollar bills he clasp in Mike's hand, acting as he were his best friend. Needless to say, Mike suddenly hit a winning streak and became excited and overconfident. His winning streak didn't last long. He lost his winnings plus the three 10's Sergeant Wood had handed him. The Sarge was kneeled beside Mike with one hand on the boy's shoulder still encouraging him to continue as he placed another $30 in the boy's hand. He rubbed up and down over Mike's back assuring him that this time the strategy would work and he would start winning again. The sergeant kept reassuring Mike as he continued to play. Mike started winning tosses of the dice again. Each time he did the Sarge would more aggressively run his big hand somewhere over Mike body as encouragement. However, eventually Mike's luck changed again and he started to loose. He had been so excited with the winning streak that he just continued playing until suddenly he realized he was completely out of money again. By this time Sarge had handed Michael a total $85 of his own money. Sarge tried to hand him more cash, but the kid finally wised up and refused the offer.

============

What you have to understand here is the fact that weeks earlier, the sergeant was one of the big good looking black guys that Mike found particularly attractive and had stared at in the showers. The Sarge had noticed him staring at him too, and quickly propositioned Mike a number of times trying to lure him into his private room. Of course Mike slept down at the end of the hallway in a large open room separated into many small cubicles where all the lower ranking enlisted men bunked. Each time the Sarge had propositioned Mike, he had been unsuccessful in luring Mike into his private room.

Sarge was a single man, Regular Army (RA), a career soldier in his middle 30's and one of the best looking black guys that Mike had seen in the showers, but he just couldn't allow himself to partake even though the Sarge made Mike's heart flutter and his crotch tingle, especially when he would corner Mike in the hallway to talk. The Sarge knew the kid liked him and had been checking him out, especially his big black dick in the showers. He began watching for the boy coming down the hallway past the open door to his private room. The Sarge would step out, usually shirtless and get the boy in a conversation. Sarge towered over him by almost eight inches and easily backed him into the hallway wall with his closeness. Sarge would support himself against the wall with one arm over Mike's shoulder, leaning into him so close and intimate Mike could smell the male pheromones coming off him and feel his hot breath on his face making small talk. He would work his leg and inner thigh against Michael's leg and rub it gently against the boy. Sarge's huge endowment would snake down inside his fatigue pants and rub against the boy. Michael would get all flustered and nervous as Sarge kept repositioning himself so his boner would be in constant contact with the boy. All this time the Sarge would interject sexy talk directed to Michael in his conversation. Sarge was able to get Michael nervous and sexually excited quickly and sometimes he would almost talk Mike into entering his private room with him, but Mike, though excited and turned on to the big guy, always seemed to be able to resist the temptation, though difficult, and scoot away to the safety of numbers in his own sleeping quarters.

One night after Mike started taking his shower well after midnight each night when the showers were always empty, Sarge surprised him when he walked in, turned on the spray head right next to Mike and started showering. After he was wet and lathered well in soapsuds, he turned off his shower head, faced Mike and began jacking his huge black dick into a full blown hard-on covered in soapsuds. Mike watched out of the corner of his eye for awhile, turned away slightly and tried to ignore him, but his dick gave him away when it started to harden, tingle and expand. Michael tried to rush through his shower and get rinsed and out, but the sergeant suddenly pulled Mike out from under the shower spray and pulled him up against him locked in his strong arms. He boldly began rubbing his soapy body and cock up and down between Mike's buns, holding him tightly against him until his huge black cock was pulsating with each heartbeat, pressed between the softness of the boy's firm bubble buns.

Mike was startled and tried to escape at first, but slowly succumbed to the pleasure as he relaxed also hard and sexually excited. Once Sarge began to tweak Mike's nipples he found himself paralyzed with lust undulating back against the big muscular guy. Sarge worked his slick soapy hard cock up and down between the boy's buns and dropped one soapy hand from Mike's nipples to the boy's cock and began to jack him slowly as he continued to rub his cock between the boy's hot buns. He put his huge lips against Mike's neck and nibbled his way up to suck on the boy's earlobe. Sarge whispered softly, "Just relax and enjoy baby!" Sarge soon exploded his hot juices clear up over Mike's back, shoulders and neck. Seconds later Michael trembled, stiffened and climaxed into Sarge's hand where he had the head of his dick clasp in the soft folds of his palm rubbing the tender glands where he had been gently stroking the boy. Mike's legs went limp and he started to fall to his knees as he climaxed, but Sarge held him up until he was able to regain the ability to stand on his own again. Sarge returned the boy under his shower head and washed his juices from the kid's backside. Sarge turned his own shower head back on and they finished their shower, stepped out and dried watching each other. Not a single word was spoken.

Sarge was standing looking at himself in the mirror over a sink shaving his head and goatee when Mike came out from one of the toilet enclosures. They locked eyes in the mirror as Sarge gave him a wink. Mike's turned red with embarrassment, dropped his eyes to the floor, grabbed his stuff and departed.

The next day Mike was back taking his shower as usual when they were filled with guys, knowing better than be caught alone again in the showers by the Sarge or anyone else; though he knew he wanted more of that big guy making love to him. Maybe that's why his subconscious mind later drew him into that crap game where he knew Sarge would either be playing or watching from the sidelines. He also knew he could have just left when he started to loose his own money, but he didn't. Then to let the Sarge talk him back into the game and front $85 had him thinking he either had to be crazy insane or crazy wanting to be touched and receive some more attention from the big black hunk enough to let it all happen subconsciously.

===========

After Mike lost the $85 of Sarge's money, Sarge escorted him off to the side and told him that he would have to either immediately pay up or go with him to his room and settle his debt by putting out, as he expected the debt to be paid back one way or the other. Mike made a few requests to borrow the $85 from some of the guys that were in the game that he knew, but they just looked up at him and laughed as Sarge waited for him at his side with his big hand placed on the boy's awesome derriere gently patting, rubbing and squeezing his new boy.

Staff Sergeant Axel Wood's arm was around Mike's waist holding him up next to him the second the final request for an $85 loan was rejected. Sarge turned and squeezed his family jewels to the group huddled on the floor watching them depart, letting them all know by the gesture that he was taking possession of Mike and planned to make him his new conquest. The minute the sergeant had Mike halfway up the stairs on the landing headed for his second floor room, he moved his hand down from Mike's waist and began to squeeze the boy's buns as he guided him along. Once on the second floor he continued to guide Mike along the hallway to the door to his own private room. He opened it with his passkey, guiding Mike into his private domain and locked the door with the deadbolt. He immediately pulled Mike into his arms, ruffled his soft blond locks and looked down into his light gray/blue eyes and smiled.

Sarge whispered, "No more denying me what I've been wanting for a good long time now. Your pretty white ass is mine now baby!"

Sarge released Michael knowing he wouldn't dare try to escape. Sarge unbuttoned his shirt, removed it, and tossed it on a chair, which left him nude from the waist up. He had been sweating and his black muscled torso and six-pack glistened like fresh pumped crude oil. He flipped the radio on to a reggae station, adjusted the volume, and turned his attention back to Michael. He flexed his biceps and made his abs ripple as Mike watched. Sarge began to strut his stuff around Mike, the kind of sexy strut we have all seen that black guys do when they are excited or showing off to their women, all in time to the music. He was loosening his belt and undoing the buttons on his fly as his strut continued. Suddenly he stopped strutting facing directly in front of Mike, lifted his entire package, cock and balls and let them dangle and sway as he rotated his hips and undulated from the waist as though he was fucking. Mike mouth was agape watching as the black monster dick started to come alive, thicken and lift off the low hanger ball sacks. As it grew, the long foreskin umbrella pulled back slowly, displaying the huge purple head and massive mushroomed glands where they attached to the black shaft. It was so huge it could only make it up to about a 45 degree angle. He began to tweak his nipples and the big huge veined monster started to twitch and pulsate as he got his abs rippling again. He went back into his strut mode and danced around Mike. Mikes eyes were glued to him as he continued his sexy strut. His cock was now leaking copious amounts of pre-cum. The strut suddenly stopped again, as he stood back about three feet directly in front of Mike again.

Sarge softly said, "Now get nude boy and stand at attention so I can look you over real good."

Mike continued to stand in the middle of the room frozen, watching him without moving, as though he was in a trance or hypnotized. Sarge could see the boy was sporting a hard-on, as his fatigues pants were tented to the hilt. The kid was obviously going commando, as a wet spot was forming at the top of the tent.

"Damn Boy, I said GET NUDE, and do it now before you cream yourself! Don't make me hurt you boy to do as I say! DO YOU HEAR ME BOY?"

Mike came out of his stupor, looked down at his wet spot, then his feet and said almost apologetically, "I can't do that Sarge. Please, just let me go and I will pay you back double, some each payday. Sarge, I'm a Virgin Christian Boy and can't be doing this!"

Sarge was on him like a bolt of lightning. He backhanded the boy across the face twice and said louder than normal, "YOU BEST GET OUT OF THOSE DUDS BOY, RIGHT NOW!"

Mike was stunned by the harsh unexpected backhand and the sudden dominant tone in the sergeant's voice. He put a hand to his jaw and worked it back and forth trying to relieve the pain the blow caused. He realized the Sarge meant business when a swift jab to his abs folded him in the middle sending him flying back against the cinder-block far wall which left him in a heap on the cold tile floor.

Sarge continued, "Now you best be undressed and standing at attention by the time I get my boots off, undressed and drinks poured, and I don't want to hear another word from you other than 'YES SARGE' or 'NO SARGE' when I ask you something, YOU HEAR ME BOY?"

Mike looked up from the floor at the sergeant, his eyes moist with tears, and whimpered, "Yes Sarge!" He knew now for sure Sarge meant business. Mike worked his way back to his feet again and started to undress, throwing his clothing on the chair next to Sarge's desk where Sarge had thrown his shirt earlier. He barely was able to get his clothing and boots off before the Sarge was standing facing his locker rummaging through things looking for something as he undressed completely.

The Sarge was totally nude when he found what he was looking for and pulled the items off the shelves, turned and set them on the desktop. He opened a desk drawer and pulled a bottle of liquor and two shot glasses and a couple of other items and added them up topside. Sarge was at least 6'6", huge muscles, even large for a black man. His head was shaved, but his body had tuffs of curly black hair across his chest and down over his body. He had a thin goatee. His pits and groin were a mass of kinky black longer hair. A massive cock was still semi-hard and swung like a huge black pendulum with his every move. Two large eggs hung in their smooth hairless low hangers, one a bit longer than the other. They swung from side to side slapping against his inner thighs as he poured Wild Turkey into the two shot glasses. When Sarge turned around Mike was standing at attention in the middle of the room watching his every move, eyes still watered over.

Sarge stepped up to Mike and rubbed his hands all over his body as though checking the merchandise for any flaws, imperfections, or irregularities. He lifted the boy's uncircumcised cock and balls and gave them a few pulls until the cock returned to semi-hard and started to grow even larger in his hand. He worked the skin back and forth over the head a few times. He tweaked Mike's large nipples with the other hand and continued to jack the loose skin on and off the moist pink head stroking the boy to a full hard-on. The pre-cum oozed from the tip of his perfectly formed cock. He ran his thumb thru the slick and spread it over the surface of the pretty pink cock head and around the sensitive glands. The boy let out a soft moan and began to tremble uncontrollably. It was obvious he liked these new feelings of lust and was letting them ripple through his body. He leaned forward slightly toward Sarge almost falling out of attention until Sarge grabbed him by the balls and squeezed them hard until the boy was standing on his toes and his dick was flaccid again.

Sarge removed his hands from the boy's cock and balls and grabbed him by the nips, pinched, twisted and tweaked them until they were standing like two quarter inch pink buttons on half dollar size slightly darker pink areolas. The boy let out another moan and his cock started to stiffen up again. Sarge was boning up himself as he leaned into the boy and sucked on his nipples. The pre-cum started flowing again from the boy's cock slit. Sarge grabbed a gob of the boy's pre on his middle finger and went behind the boy, spread his buns and rubbed the slick on his pinkie. The boy flinched and almost fell out from attention again, caught himself and tried to stand perfectly still as Sarge reached between his legs and pulled his cock so he could milk more pre-cum on to his finger. He continued rubbing pre-cum on the pinkie until he had it well lubed. He then milked more pre-cum on to his finger and began to work the finger into Mike's anus. The boy was tight, but soon began to relax and let the finger enter, massage and rotate. Sarge was searching for the boy's prostrate gland. When Sarge located and gave the little hard walnut a few pokes the boy let out a moan and started to drip more pre-cum. Sarge continued to massage and poke until Michael's legs were trembling and his body shaking. He was about to climax had Sarge not removed his finger and slapped the boy hard a couple of times across the ass.

"Well! I see everything is in working order boy and you seem to be a hot little fucker back here, but I don't want you shooting off until I tell you that you can boy. It's time for a couple of drinks and an Ecstasy pill for you boy. That should help loosen you up and get you all turned on to this nigger's big licorice stick. You're virginity really excites me boy. I can't believe no one has popped your cherry ass yet. You're so fucking beautiful, just like a blond virgin maiden." Sarge came around and stuck his wet finger in Mike's mouth and said, "Suck it clean Boy!" The boy complied without hesitation.

Sarge returned to the desk, grabbed the two jiggers of Wild Turkey and a pill. He downed the one drink and set the empty back on the desk. He stepped over in front of Mike, and forced his mouth open with his fingers, dropped the pill on his tongue and put the jigger of Wild Turkey to the boy's lips.

"Down the hatch boy and swallow that pill." After the boy swallowed the Wild Turkey Sarge told him to open his mouth wide as he ran his long black index finger around inside his mouth to make sure he had swallowed the Ecstasy pill as told. He found it hidden, lodged under the boy's tongue. He retrieved the pill and said, "Just as I expected. You don't want to get me upset again boy and end up on the floor with a sore belly ache!" He refilled the jigger with Wild Turkey, held the boy's head back with his mouth wide open, tossed the pill back down his throat and quickly poured the Wild Turkey in and held the boy by the chin until he swallowed the pill this time. Again, he checked to make sure the boy had truly swallowed the pill. "Good Boy! You can stand at ease now"

The boy relaxed and followed Sarge with his eyes as he returned to the drawer of the desk and pulled out what looked to be a cigarette. He lit it up and took a couple of long drags and then put it to the boy's lips and told him to puff. The boy shook his head no until Sarge back handed him again. "You never smoked pot before, have you boy?"

"No Sarge!"

"Well this doesn't have any nicotine in it, so it won't hurt you. It will calm your nerves. Now let's try this again!" He put the roach to the boy's lips again and the boy knew better than experience another harder backhand. He took a short drag on the reefer and immediately started coughing. After the kid recovered Sarge said, "Damn Boy! This time just suck the smoke down quickly, without hesitating and you won't start coughing like that. Here goes." He put it to the boy's lips and he inhaled it quickly like he was instructed. He didn't cough this time, but blew the smoke right back out into the room and made a nasty face indicating it tasted horrible. "This time inhale it and hold it in your lungs as long as you can boy. Here goes now." Mike inhaled the smoke and held it in as long as he could and Sarge gave him a little peck on the lips with his own before he said with a smile, "That's my boy!" Sarge took another long drag on the reefer and then began passing it back and forth sharing it with the boy. "Good stuff boy, give us a good buzz here shortly. You'll love the calming that will take place!" He kissed the boy again completely covering the boy's lips with his big thick lips and running his tongue around inside the boy's mouth. He could see the boy was beginning to loosen up and respond to his attentions, so he grabbed another reefer from the drawer, lit it up and passed it back and forth until it too had to be hooked on the roach clip to finish off. Another jigger each of Wild Turkey and the boy was responding well to the kisses, the little nibbles and the pecks on his ears and neck and the rubbing along his inner thighs.

When Sarge raised one of his arms and put Mike's nose into the fragrant wet pit hair the boy relaxed and began to inhale the strong masculine scent. The male pheromones filled his nasal passages. Mike's tongue was soon busy tasting the moisture and his nose was inhaling the aroma. It was clear that he was enjoying both the taste and the masculine scent of the pit. Sarge moved him to his other pit and continued this very important new experience for the boy. He then worked the boy lips over his nipples and down the center of his chest over his six pack abs and into the mass of hair surrounding the huge black dick, pushing the boy down on to his knees. It too was dripping wet with huge amounts of clear pre-cum oozing from his piss-slit.

Sarge whispered, "Kiss it baby! Soon it will be your new best friend and your favorite new sex toy, the love of your life!" He gently pushed it to the boy's lips and rubbed the copious amount of pre-cum it was producing back and forth over his lips. "Put your tongue out boy and taste of it!" Slowly the tongue came out from between pink lips and made a quick dip into the sauce and quickly receded back into hiding. "Again now boy, let's see that pretty pink tongue taste some more!" The boy was looking up at Sarge with dreamy eyes now as the tongue emerged again and lapped into the sauce. Sarge realized the booze, the pot and possibly even the Ecstasy were kicking in when Mike smiled up into his eyes and started to kiss, lick and suck up the sweet nectar.

"Good Boy! Now work the skin back and run your tongue around and under the head as you suck on more of the shaft babe! Mmmm! Oh Yea, just like that baby! You love that salty sweet taste and the strong smell of a black man don't you baby?"

"Mmmm! Mmmm!"

A soft knock on the door brought Sarge back awake. He gave Mike a shake to wake him up, then jumped to his feet and walked to the door and asked, "Who's there?"

CHAPTER TWO

"It's me, Rolf! Open up bro! I've come to collect!" The deadbolt clanked and Sarge opened the door just a crack to make sure that Rolf was alone, then opened it a bit more, enough to barely let Rolf enter. He quickly closed and reset the deadbolt.

Rolf said, "Damn bro its dark in here, turn on a light or light a candle or something."

Sarge said, "Mother-Fuck, we must have fallen asleep." He flipped on a small reading light sitting on his desk. He was rubbing his eyes when he said, "Give me a minute or two bro, at the moment I'm stupefied, my brain isn't working yet!" Michael was sitting up off his back slightly supported by his elbows, looking as though he was in nana land sporting a full boner, sticking straight up in the air dripping with pre-cum as Rolf's eyes adjusted to the low light in the room enough to see Michael in full display.

Rolf commented, "Ain't he something alright, a real looker! Just look at the juice flowing from the cracker's dick. Not a bad size either, for a white boy! How are his cock-sucking abilities Sarge?"

"Fuck bro, he's a natural, learned to take all my 12" in one easy lesson after I got some Wild Turkey down him, we smoked a couple of joints, and the Ecstasy I gave him kicked in a bit. He's hot and ready to take all the way from virgin-boy to pussy-boy status. Business first bro - you bring my $85?

"Sure enough - a deal's a deal Sarge." He pulled out a large roll of greenbacks he had rubber banded and stuffed in his coat pocket, slid the rubber band off the wad, counted out $85 and handed it to Sarge. He rolled up and re-banded the wad and returned it to his coat pocket and remarked, "Damn did I fleece them white boys of their money tonight. The dice were good to me tonight. I got me better than $250 in that wad of cash, and would have had damn near twice that, except bro Jerald from E Company came along after you two left. That mother-fucker hit a winning streak and ended up with about another $180 that should have been all mine."

Rolf stepped over to Mike and ran a hand through his soft golden hair and said, "Damn he is one hot looking blond cracker bro. I'll take any part of him you're willing to share with me after I collect what you already owe me. Fuck, I should have held out for a piece of his fine cracker ass too along with the blow job. Damn bro, just lookin at the bitch givin me a boner!" His hand went to his crotch and readjusted himself before taking his coat off and throwing it in the corner, kicking off his boots, pulling his wife beater off over his head, dropping his fatigues along with his army issue whites and tossed them all into the pile.

He swiftly jumped up onto the bed with Mike and was all over the kid in a flash, licking, sucking nipples and rubbing himself all over the boy. Then he flipped Mike over on his stomach, spread his legs out wide and buried his face between the awesome buns lapping his tight pink rosebud. He lifted his face up and looked over at Sarge and said, "He's all slick back here, but tighter than a drum. Ain't you fucked him yet man?"

"Meant to Rolf, but guess we fell asleep before I got to it. I'm pretty fucked up too myself - a little too much Wild Turkey maybe."

"Well Sarge, Good! I'll just be warming him up for you then bro. He's pretty tight down here, sure to be a virgin, but old magic tongue will have him all loosened up for you lick-ah-de-split. Damn man, he smells good, taste even better – not a hair one down here and nice and clean. Is that Mary Jane I smell in here, sure smell like that to me bro?"

Sarge answered, "Yea, I scored some off base earlier after we got paid this morning along with a bottle of amyl nitrate and some Ecstasy pills. The pots not bad shit, but I've had much better. I haven't tried the amyl, plan to use it on the kid to really get that pussy gyrating on my dick once I get him opened up. If you can tear yourself away from that tasty muffin, I'll share a couple reefers with you bro."

"Give me a few minutes yet bro; this is way too tasty a morsel to abandon until I get my tongue inside this tight rosebud and get me a good taste of his sweet nectar. It smells like Irish Spring, tastes like walnuts, licorice and someone's pre-cum so far. Mmmm, this one is extra special – nice and sweet, smooth as glass, soft like a baby ass and the prettiest pink as you could ever want! What a rush!" He continued to work on Mike until the little guy was moaning and raising his ass up pushing it hard against his face. Rolf's head popped up and announced, "I'm in bro and the coast is clear as far as this magic tongue will reach." He dove back in and really began munching in the honey pot. He rose up again and declared, "He's beginning to dilate, but he's definitely a virgin and is going to take a lot of lube and pre-cum to get him ready for the plunge with that monster dick of yours. Woof! I think I'm ready for a little smoke now. A shot or two of that there Wild Turkey would be great too buddy, if you're in the giving mood tonight!" He flipped Mike back over on his back, popped a sloppy kiss on his lips and hopped off the bed.

Mike moaned, "Why did you stop doing that Sarge, it felt really great?" When he took a better look at Rolf in the dim light he declared, "You aren't Sarge! Who are you anyway?" He paused looking at Rolf a moment. "Oh yea, I know who you are. You're Rolf, the guy that won all my pay, but that's alright because Sarge is going to take care of me and let me suck his big dick some more. You know, he taught me to swallow it and I love it. He tastes really good like warm, creamy pudding. You want me to suck your cock? Sarge said I was a natural cock-sucker? You're a real looker too, but not really, really handsome like Sarge and your cock definitely not as big as his either, but way bigger than mine. I'd like to see it nice and hard. You get it hard and I'll suck it for you. Would you like that, huh Rolf?" Mike was talking louder than normal and slurring his words.

Rolf piped up, "Put a cork in it Mikie! You're rambling like a drunken bitch in heat! You'll get some of this nigger's dick later honey –

not to worry!" He turned to Sarge who was sitting in the dark lighting up a joint and said, "I think your honey has had just a bit too much Wild Turkey tonight; maybe a few hits on that joint will calm her down a bit before she wakes the neighborhood with her drunken ramblings."

Sarge jumped to his feet and stepped out of the dark up to the bed and back handed Mike across the face gently to get his full attention, "Now shut the fuck up Baby, or I'll gag you with my dirty stinking socks and put you on latrine duty with the other fuck ups come Monday morning." He stuck the joint between Mike lips and told him to take a good long hit and hold it in his lungs as long as he could. He waited for the kid to exhale and breathe for a minute. He put it to Mike's lips and told him to do it again, then turned, took a big hit off it and passed it to Rolf and said, "Finish it off bro." He poured Rolf a shot of Wild Turkey. After Rolf finished off the reefer clasped in the clip, he downed the straight shot of Wild Turkey.

Out of the corner of Sarge's eye he saw Mike was slowly stroking himself. He quickly stepped over to the bed and pulled the kids hand from his dick and glared down at him and said, "Didn't I tell you that you couldn't do that until I said you could Baby? Now keep your hand off your dick and calm down!"

Mike wined, "Yes Sarge, I think I forgot – but I'm really horny and need to cum or something. I'm all nervous and my insides are on fire, even my ass is twitching where Rolf was licking and sucking. Please help me calm down Sarge, be near me! Hold me! I've never felt this way before. What's wrong with me?"

Sarge smiled down at Michael, leaned over and kissed him gently on the lips and said, "It's the Ecstasy pill doing its thing to make you real horny Babe! Don't you worry, Rolf and I are going to fix you right up and make you feel real good soon." He turned his head to Rolf and said, "The timings perfect – Cherry Picking Time has arrived! Get up here bro and warm him up again."

Rolf responded, "Gladly! Won't take much more and he will be in the zone and his ass itching and pulsating with the need for something bigger than my tongue and fingers. You sure you don't want your buddy here to break him in for you first?"

"Fuck, no way Rolf, I've been waiting to do this for way to long already. No more cat and mouse games. His cock teasing days, wiggling his hot ass around us are over. I've been having dreams about this unveiling for weeks. You're going to keep him quiet with that black skin flute like I promised you while I pop his cherry ass. Maybe later I'll let you have sloppy seconds, if you keep him good and quiet and he is moaning for more ass play after I drop my seed in him and Bust his Cherry."

"Oh great Sarge, you know I'll keep him quiet, you just gave me the incentive. A blow-jobs great, but riding that bubble butt would be fucking fantastic buddy."

"Now help me slide the bed out away from the wall about two feet so we can work him together from both ends," Sarge said. The three-quarter bed sat high off the floor, a perfect height for tall guys. It slid easily, even with Mike aboard. Sarge continued, "I'll set this lube, the amyl, this towel and clean pair of sock on the bed where we can reach them. Now get your black ass up there and do your thing again while I light up another joint for us. Get him all warmed up real good, dilated and well lubed so I can go pearl diving."

"Yes Boss Man!" Rolf jumped up on the bed, flipped Mike over on his stomach, spread his legs apart and went back in with his magic tongue again as Sarge stepped back to the desk and rolled few joints.

Sarge was soon back standing at the edge of the bed with another lit reefer in his mouth. He started sharing it with both Mike, by holding his head up and turning it so he could toke, and putting it to Rolf's lips every time he came up for a breather. When the last of the joint was gone, Sarge lifted Mike's head up to the side and let him suck on the head of his dick getting it dripping with pre-cum and hard again.

It didn't take long and Michael had his ass raised up slightly in the air, moaning softly, wanting more tongue, more slick fingers in him with deeper penetration. Rolf removed his face and was pumping and spinning four long fingers in the boy's pulsating honey pot when he eventually pulled them out and spoke.

"Sarge, he's as ready as he's going to get for the master's touch." Sarge pulled his dick from Mike's mouth, and passed it over to Rolf who lubed it up well and the two moved Michael crosswise on the bed with his legs up in the air. Sarge slipped between the legs, lifted them up on his shoulders and Rolf guided Sarge's huge cock to the cavern entrance, lining the head up for the big plunge. Rolf quickly scurried around to the other side of the bed and fed his cock into Michael's mouth, readjusting the boy's head so it laid back over the edge of the bed at a perfect angle to slide his expanding cock right in and easily deep throat the boy. He gave Sarge the high sign to go ahead holding Mike's head tightly between his thighs, balls resting over nose and eyes to keep him in place and quiet.

Sarge suddenly lunged right from his hips and his huge purple cock-head popped through the sphincter muscle in one quick move. The head was in alright, but Mike stiffened and began to convulse. Sarge stopped right there. The boy tried to scream out his pain and shake himself free from their clutches. His efforts were futile. The tears rolled from his eyes and a sudden look of horror spread over his face. Rolf had Mike's mouth stuffed with cock to keep him from screaming, trying to calm the boy by stroking his head and wiping the tears from his eyes with a clean sock. After a minute or so the boy began to relax around what must have felt like a red hot poker or a fireball had entered him. Sarge began the slow descent into the tight burning cavern. Little by little, he worked more and more into the boy as Rolf kept the boy occupied sucking on his cock. The boy was trembling and sweat was forming on his extremities as little by little Sarge fed more of his huge, shinny black meat into the tight orifice.

Suddenly, almost like magic, Michael's eyes brightened, and he let out a little moan looking up into Rolf's eyes. He began to rotate and hump his buns, a sure sign that Sarge had made contact with the boy's hard little walnut and it was beginning to feel good. The Sarge rotated his cock-head on the spot for awhile, then gradually worked the remaining length of his 12 inches into the boy's bottom and began to rotate, knead and loosen the boy's tight virgin honey pot. Soon he was taking short strokes, gradually increasing their length until he was working the entire black veined shaft from cock-head down to his pubes, in and out, rubbing and massaging Michael's hard little nutty walnut.

Rolf was actively pumping his full ten inches down the boy's throat. Mike was spewing copious amounts of pre-cum all over his own stomach and chest moaning with excitement. It didn't take very long and the three were lusting and having the time of their life sharing with each other the pleasures of the flesh. All three were in the zone – time had stopped – emotions were high – their fluids were boiling and about to erupt.

Rolf was the first to stiffen, shudder and shoot. He pumped two shots of baby makers down the boy's throat directly into his stomach, pulled his cock-head back into the boy's mouth and unloaded the balance into his mouth. The large volume of jizz oozed from the corners of his mouth, ran down his jaws and drop as a web to the floor. Rolf kept his dick in Michael's mouth to guarantee his silence.

Michael was the second to tremble with excitement, experiencing his very first anal induced orgasm, covering himself from chin to chest with his own sweet nectar. The boy's sphincter muscle pulsated around Sarge's massive endowment. Sarge, though he tried, could hold his climax back no longer. His legs began to tremble and shudder. His whole body stiffened as he buried his cock into Michael's bottom and was virtually milked of his hot nigger jizz by the kid's throbbing anus muscles.

Michael's pussy-lips continued to throb, beat and pulsate with the rhythm of his quickened heartbeat along the long black shaft of the Sarge's huge cock, keeping him hard, excited and lusting for more of the pleasures within this awesome white ass. There was no holding back as Sarge began to fuck the boy a second time. Rolf kept putting the bottle of amyl-nitrate to the nose of both Michael and the Sarge, sending them into periods of uncontrollable spasmodic undulations until they both had one orgasm after the other.

Sarge finally was able to clear his head enough to utter, "Enough Rolf, I can't take any more!" Rolf stopped administering the amyl and Sarge pulled his cock from Mike, lay across the bed and slowly came down from his high as his blood pressure returned to normal. Michael's legs were now down over the edge of the bed, but he was still undulating and rolling his ass against the towel Rolf had thrown under his ass to catch any jizz that might seep from his well dilated anus.

Sarge was dripping wet with perspiration, as was Michael. Rolf was standing watching them both, yet sporting a big boner again. Sarge rose to his feet and slowly hobbled to the desk, grabbed a cigarette and the lighter and flopped in the chair and lit it up. He spread his legs out wide in front of himself and watched Michael and Rolf. Rolf was looking down at Michael slowly stroking himself and running his fingers through

Michael's golden locks admiring the beautiful boy. Michael was still humping his buns against the mattress, moaning and trying to reach with one hand for Rolf's boner with a gapping open mouth. The fingers on his other hand were pinching and pulling on his own nipples.

Rolf looked over at Sarge and asked, "How about letting me fuck him now Sarge. He's still humping his buns, grabbing for my hard cock and horny for some more action?"

Sarge gave Rolf a big smile and said, "Here's the deal bro. You give the kid back his $59 dollars and I'll let you fuck him, but every time you want to screw him in the future it is going to cost you $20 and $10 for a blowjob. Take it or leave it buddy."

"Well you Mother Fucker! That's how you repay your bro - the buddy that helped you set the kid up earlier. He wouldn't be here now if it weren't for me!"

"Like I said bro, take it or leave it! That's the discounted price I'll be giving my buddies and special friends. I could charge you full price for this choice beef, and haven't I shared my liquor and pot with you tonight already. I'd say you're getting off cheap bro."

Rolf looked down at Michael's luscious body and watched him for a minute or so, then said, "OK Sarge, you got a deal, but don't expect too get off this cheap next time you want to pull another honky white ass cracker into your web." He came around from the other side of the bed and retrieved the roll of cash from his fatigue jacket, counted out the $59 and put it on the desk, rolled and put the rest back in his jacket and tossed it back into the pile.

Rolf was on Michael in a flash, rolling him over on the bed lengthwise on his stomach. He climbed behind Michael, held his head down against the bed and lifted his ass up with the other until the boy was in the doggie position. He placed the towel on the bed under the boy to catch any mess he might make and entered him in one swift motion. He fucked the kid like there was no tomorrow, slowing when he started to get close to climax, speeding up when he came back down. He grabbed the amyl and gave both Michael and himself a good whiff of the strong smelling liquid and they both went into convulsive muscle spasms, pounding, pulsating and beating against each other until Rolf could hold back no longer and they both reached a roaring climax. Michael went flat over the bed, Rolf covering him with his sweaty body as he nibbled and sucked on his neck, shoulder and earlobe.

Sarge piped up, "Don't you be putting any marks on my boy bro. You got what you came here for; so get your nigger ass off him, get dressed and get the fuck on your way now. It's after midnight and time for his hot shower and beauty rest."

Rolf dressed and left in total silence. Sarge got Michael on his feet, grabbed a couple of towels, wrapped them around them, grabbed a bar of soap and marched Michael down the hallway the short distance to the bathroom and into the large shower stall. Sarge was hung over pretty bad and not in a playful mood, but Michael was still full of piss and vinegar, the Ecstasy obviously still working on him. As Sarge had him under the hot steaming water trying to wash them both, Michael was constantly trying to grab Sarge's cock and play with it. Sarge finally got discussed with the kid and gave him a couple of hard smacks on his ass and told him to cool it. It only turned Michael on more. The kid dropped to his knees and sucked up Sarge's cock quicker than grease lightening and Sarge's cock responded immediately. He got a raging hard-on again quickly and succumbed to the pleasure.

Sarge backed himself up against the wall with the warm water flowing down over them both and let the kid suck him to his heart's content, eventually spewing another big load down Michael's throat. While he was still semi-hard he lifted Mike up, turned him around and entered him. He worked his dick into the kid's bottom and slowly fucked him as he jacked the kid off and made him cum a big load down the tiled shower wall. He continued pumping as he jacked Michael through two more orgasms. Michael's fourth climax proved to be a dry orgasm. Sarge cleaned up the kid and the mess, rinsed, dried and returned them to Sarge's room.

Sarge pulled the covers back on the bed and ordered Michael into bed. He told him to calm down, relax and go to sleep. He really wanted to send the kid back to his own bed in the barracks, but he didn't know what the kid would do if on his own until he was himself again. Sarge paced the floor smoking a couple of cigarettes before he finally put things back in order in the room watching Michael, hoping he would drop off to sleep before he was finished. Finally Mike seemed to be asleep, so he turned off the light and crawled in behind, spooning him and quickly dropped off to sleep.

When Sarge awoke and looked at the clock it was going on to 7am, Michael was gone as were the boy's clothing. He rushed to dress and went to see if Michael was in his own bed in his cubicle. No Michael. He rushed down to the dining room just before they closed it down. It was almost empty except for a few guys together talking at the front of the room seated together. He looked at the very back and there was Michael alone, his back to him, eating breakfast. Sarge grabbed a tray, loaded up some breakfast, grabbed a cup of coffee and walked the full length of the dining room and sat directly across from Michael.

Michael looked up, saw Sarge, and immediately looked back down into his tray of food and said, "I'm not talking to you after what you and Rolf did to me last night. Just go away and leave me alone. I'm so sore I can hardly sit down. FUCK you both Sarge!"

Sarge whispered, "Not so loud Baby, but you know you loved it. You had the time of your life Baby! Here, I have something for you." He pulled the $59 from his pocket and set it down in front of Michael. "See, I even got your pay back from Rolf Baby Cakes. I know you like me and in a couple of days your bottom will be as good as new and you will be back for more loving. Now look up at me and give me a big smile, OK Baby! You know you're real special to me."

Michael never said another word to Sarge, just continued eating his breakfast, occasionally looking up watching the Sarge shoveling his food down to catch up with Michael. Sarge handed his empty coffee cup to Michael and told him to get him a refill. Michael hesitated for a moment, then reached across and took the cup from Sarge, rose and returned with a refill for the Sarge and another glass of hot chocolate for himself. Sarge could see from the way he walked and especially when he sat back down that the kid was obviously quite sore. Michael looked into Sarge's eyes and started to say something, quickly looked down and began to fill up emotionally. A slow trickle of tears ran down his face for a moment. He wiped them with a napkin, took another taste from his hot chocolate and just sat there staring at Sarge. Still, not a word was exchanged, but Sarge extended his hand across the table, pressed it over Michael's and squeezed it gently.

When they were finished and returning their trays to the dishwasher's window, Sarge put his arm on Michael's shoulder, gave it a little squeeze and said, "Come up to the room Baby and I'll put some ointment on your sore bottom and give you a valium. The ointment will help take the pain away and the valium will calm your nerves and make you feel better!"

"Well OK, but no more fooling around with my bottom. You promise Sarge?"

"Sure, no more fooling around with it for a few days baby. I'll get your bottom all feeling better and take you to a Sunday afternoon matinee in Tacoma this afternoon. We will get out of the barracks and you will feel much better. No more tears now Baby. Everything is going to be just fine. You'll see!"

"Well, let's see how I feel after you put the ointment on me. Right now all I want to do is curl up and die somewhere."

"Don't talk like that Baby. I'll have you all fixed up and feeling better in no time."

When they got in Sarge's room he had Michael lower his fatigues and lean over the edge of the bed. He spread his legs and checked out his pink rosebud. It was red, swollen, puffed and still a bit dilated. He grabbed the ointment from his locker and spread a gob with his finger over the rosebud. Michael flinched, but let him rub it gently over the inflamed and swollen area. He gradually worked a large amount down inside Michael's anus. It felt cool and soothing to Michael as he began to relax, the pain and burning began to subside.

After Sarge wiped his fingers clean on a towel he grabbed a Valium pill from a plastic prescription container. He placed it in Michael's mouth. He grabbed a full bottle of spring water and handed it to Michael and said, "Down the hatch Babe. It will calm you down and make you feel better. Now go down to your cubicle and nap on your bed for awhile. I'll come by and awaken you about lunch time. You can change into some civilian clothing and we will do lunch together, then we will take off to catch a matinee in Tacoma." He pulled Michael into his strong arms, planted his lips over Michael's and gave him a long juicy French kiss and headed him through the doorway and down the hallway to the barracks and his bed.

Sarge led Michael to the last row at the very top of the second tier level in the movie theatre. The valium had kicked in and Michael was calmed and somewhat spaced out watching the movie with his head laid over on Sarge's shoulder when Sarge opened up his pants and pulled out his big black pecker and placed Michael's hand over the head and gently squeezed his fingers around the shaft. He held Mike's hand in place and slowly started working the loose skin up and down over his cock head. Soon Michael was jacking him without any assistance from Sarge, so he removed his hand and let Michael continue on his own.

Sarge whispered, "Get on your knees baby and lean over and suck it!" As Michael dropped into the tight space to his knees Sarge scooted down in his seat giving Mike better access to his black beauty. It was dripping copious amounts of pre-cum and Mike was licking it up as if it were a big chocolate ice cream cone. He couldn't get much more than the head and a couple of inches in his mouth at the awkward angle, but Mike was working his tongue around the glands, licking up the steady flow of pre and jacking it with his hand. It wasn't long and Sarge let out a moan and began approaching a climax.

Sarge whispered dirty talk to Michael, affectionately calling him his pretty cocksucker and hot new pussy-boy. When Sarge couldn't hold back any longer he held Michael's mouth firmly down over his cock-head and whispered, "Here it comes, eat it Baby!" Michael gobbled Sarge's juicer down, licked his lips and creamed his own shorts in the process, as he had been rubbing his crotch against Sarge's leg all the time he was sucking the big chocolate cream-maker. Sarge pulled his pants up, buttoned and told Michael to go to the bathroom and clean himself before cum soaked through his shorts and left a big wet spot on the front of his pants.

After they left the movie theatre, Sarge drove through an old neighborhood of Tacoma that was pretty run down. He pulled up in front of an old two story Victorian that looked like it needed a lot more repairs than a coat of fresh paint could fix. Sarge turned to Michael and said, "I've got to pick up a few items from the dude that lives here. You wait in the car; I shouldn't be more than a few minutes. He eventually came back with a bag full of stuff and put it on the floorboard behind the driver's seat. They drove off heading for the base. They arrived just in time for the chow line to still be open serving dinner. After eating they went back to the car and retrieved the bag and went up to Sarge's room. Sarge set the deadbolt again and Mike asked him if he could rub more ointment on his sore bottom. Completing that task, Sarge broke another Valium pill in half and had Mike take it with a few gulps from the bottled water. The heat coming off the radiator had the room very toasty, so Sarge removed his shirt, pants, shoes and socks, hung them in his locker and told Mike to strip down to his boxers and they laid on the bed and after making out for a couple of minutes, Michael nestled up against Sarge and made a little moan. Sarge put an arm up behind his head like he had before and moved Michael's face into his armpit. Mike snuggled in closer and sniffed the strong male scent then started slowly licking and sucking up the heavy moisture. He whispered, "Oh Sarge, your smell makes me tingle." Sarge tweaked the boy's erect nipples with the fingers for awhile and soon they were both asleep.

A series of knocks on the door brought Sarge awake. He rubbed his eyes, slowly got to his feet and sauntered to the door wondering who the fuck would be knocking at his door at this hour on a Sunday night. He asked, "Yea! Who's there and what do you want?"

CHAPTER THREE

"Sarge, open up! It's Rolf, and I need to talk to you! It's only 2100 hour buddy. You can't be in bed already."

Sarge opened the door to let Rolf enter, closed it and asked, "Well, what's so fuckin important that it couldn't wait until morning – out with it?"

Rolf started, "Well, I happen to have the door open to my room early this afternoon, when I heard someone knocking on a door down the hallway. I looked at my clock and it was not quite 1400 hour. When I popped my head out to see who it was banging so loud, the guy had his back to me and I couldn't tell who it was. He was knocking on your door Sarge and shouting your name, "Axel, Axel, please let me in." Eventually he gave up, turned and headed toward the stairwell at my end of the hallway. It was then he spotted me standing in my doorway staring at him. He recognized me and rushed toward me in a flash. As he drew nearer I finally recognized him. It was Lenny, but not the Lenny I remembered from years earlier when he was discharged and we took him into Seattle and dropped him off with Jaraald. Hell Sarge, that was well over two years ago. The kid's red hair is now long, curly and flows down over his shoulders. He was always a bit effeminate before, but wait till you see him now. I got an instant boner just looking at him, especially the way he was dressed. Jaraald has turned the kid into a real beauty – what a knock-out, right down to giving him those estrogen shots that give a guy boobs, and boobs he does indeed have now. He has no body or facial hair, narrow waist, nice wide hips and a plump ass. He was wearing tight beige women's slacks and a skin tight pink v-neck silky tee shirt that really showed off his boobs and large nipples, wedge sandals and make-up. He was quite anxious and acting like a bitch in flight with something bothering him that needed resolved possibly with the muzzle of my big black dick. How I remember how he use to crave and beg us both to pump that hot ass of his full of nigger jizz. He was one of our best experiments back then. We literally turned that butch pimple faced redhead from Oklahoma into a screaming faggot in record time. It finally took both of us, the cook Kobe and Selvon in communications to keep him with enough big black cock to keep him happy. Those were good days!"

"Thank god you're in Rolf, but where the hell is Axel," he asked? I pulled him into my room, closed the door and gave him a couple of light but swift bitch swats across the face hoping to calm him down. The kid was frantic and burst into tears rubbing his face where I had struck him. He was shaking uncontrollably now and threw himself into my arms and wrapped his arms around me and held me tight.

I said, "What's wrong baby, you can tell your buddy Rolf no matter how bad it may be?" With his arms around me and his boobs rubbing against my bare chest my boner really started to throb against him. He laid a kiss on me that set my dick drooling. I had no control over my reaction to his dropping his head to my chest, inhaling deeply and sucking on my nipples. He had my shorts open and stroking me before I caught my breath. By then I just let him have his way with me. He was definitely in control. He dropped to his knees and sucked me down his throat in one quick assault, milking me with his throat muscles and cupping my balls with his two hands. He brought me quickly to a massive eruption. After the first couple of shots down his throat he pulled back and filled his mouth with the juice from my baby makers. He groaned his approval, looked up into my eyes and smiled as he milked and cleaned up the mess he made as jizz had trickled from the corners of his mouth and wet my pubes and danglers. Hell, I was still so turned on to him that I stripped him, laid him out on my bed and fucked his ass for two more rounds of uncontrollable lust that hit me like a cannonball. He is beautiful, and those big melons certainly had me munching and slobbering in their softness. His white cracker skin was clear of all the acne he once had and there wasn't a hair one on his body – smooth as a newborn kitten and smelled of vanilla extract.

After we both settled down a bit, I got him to open up and tell me what was up between him and Jaraald that was so horrific that he had to come here acting crazy, like the world was coming to an end for him and only Axel or I could make it right again. The first thing he said was that Jaraald just recently told him that we had sold him to Jaraald when he was first discharged and wanted to stick around close to the base to be near both of us, Kobe and Selvon. He said he had no idea that Jaraald was running a whorehouse from his place until he was drugged right after we left and trained as a male prostitute and put to work with the other guys and gals he had in his stable. Jaraald kept him in lock down until he could be trusted, but Jaraald grew so fond of him himself that he took him out of regular service and made him his personal boy-bitch. That's when he started him on the shots and started the process of turning him into a transvestite, a real screamer, as Jaraald is bi and likes his boys absolutely effeminate and with big boobs, sensitive nipples, and constantly horny for his big cock. He had to be dressed as a girl at all times and the girls taught him how to sit, walk and act like a female. The shots also cleared his skin of acne and got rid of most the body hair. The rest was removed with electrolysis. He said he grew to love and adore Jaraald quickly, especially that dominant, assertive personality and the huge cock that made him feel like he couldn't live without it up his ass giving him pleasures beyond imagination, and definitely something he couldn't now live without until Jaraald laid a new plan for him this last week.

Seems that Jaraald has heard of a doctor in Mexico that does operations to remove a guys dick and sew his balls up inside so there is nothing except a little nub left to pee through, something like a woman, only he still has his balls and prostrate gland intact. That way, the guy can only ejaculate when fucked to orgasm by a guy, making him totally dependent on his partner to take him to orgasm through anal penetration, squirting his ejaculate out through the little nub that remains visible. He told Lenny that he was already in contact with the doctor and they were flying down to Mexico City in two weeks to have the necessary surgery performed.

Lenny told Jaraald that since he was taking the shots regularly and on the pills to calm him down when he got over emotional, his dick was non-functional anyway, so why have it removed since it was so very small anyway. He begged Jaraald until he was blue in the face, but Jaraald was not about to change his mind. This is the reason he had come to talk with you Axel and me. The kid is upset, scared and afraid of getting turned into a freak and then dumped by Jaraald for a real woman that can bare children and has a real pussy. Lenny even argued that he would rather become a transsexual than have this other alternative, but Jaraald had told him that his cock was way to small to mold into something that could accommodate his 14" cock, so that was out of the question.

Rolf said, "Anyway, about 1600 hour Lenny said he had to get back to Seattle before Jaraald missed him, but he was hoping that you and I would drive up and talk with Jaraald this coming Saturday or Sunday. I told him we really wouldn't be able to change his mind, besides it would only piss Jaraald off that he had been in contact with us on the subject. He then realized that I was probably right, asked if he could take a shower and clean up and we both went to the showers together. I fucked his pretty ass again with him shoved up against the tile wall under the warm water spraying on us from the showerhead, then we went back to the room, we dressed, I walked him to Jaraald's new BMW and he left. Damn what a beauty he has turned out to be too. You will be impressed when you see him again. Maybe you should talk with Jaraald and find out about getting Michael started on those shots to give him some boobs too, as Lenny said it took about a year for them to develop enough to be noticeable and they had to be strap down when he dressed as a boy until they grew large enough that it became impossible for him to hide them any longer. He said he loved his new breasts, they were very sensitive and he loved to have them fondled, licked, sucked and even fucked between. Now doesn't that sound like a great addition you could add to Michael's already glorious body?"

"Well, it sounds like you had a good time this afternoon bro. I'll give that idea some thought alright! Maybe I should take Michael by Jaraald's place this coming weekend and let him see Lenny and Jaraald. Give us both a chance to see what Michael could become if I decide to pursue turning him into a woman in the future. He's still asleep, that Valium I gave him really knocked him out after we got back from the theatre in Tacoma. I'll see what Mr. Lowe, the big man says about starting him on

34

estrogen shots after I let him know I have popped his cherry and he is well on his way to stardom as our new pussy-boy extraordinaire. Thanks for the update on Lenny; I guess I owe you another couple of freebies with Miss Michael for handling that situation with Lenny. He was always a great lay, like so many before him. Such a tiny dick though, made you wonder how he would ever be anything but a pussy-boy. Off with you now buddy. See you in the morning at roll call and breakfast."

About 0300 hour Michael awoke, sniffed at Sarge's masculine body, buried his nose in his pit again for a moment, then crawled out of bed, grabbed his clothing and returned to his own cubicle and crawled into bed until the bell rang at 0530 hour. Monday went as any other day, except he was still pretty sore and favored his bottom-side. He noticed that Sarge kept a keen eye on him most of the day as he worked and spent a lot of time with the Warrant Officer, a Mr. Lowe, that headed the personnel department where they both worked. Mr. Lowe called Michael up to his desk a couple of times asking him questions about his work and if he liked working in the department he was assigned. Just after lunch Mr. Lowe called him up to his desk again and handed him a ten dollar bill and his car keys and told him to drive off base and get him a box of the tiny Cigarillo Cigars he smoked. When he returned he noticed that his desk had been moved up front, but off to the side where Mr. Lowe had full view of him at all times.

As he handed the box of Cigarillo Cigars to Mr. Lowe, his hand was grabbed and held onto as the big man told him he was promoting him to be his personal assistant and secretary, what his duties would be and that he expected him to follow his orders to the tee and his new rank would be SP-4 with an increase from $59 to $119 per month. Sarge was standing off to the side smiling at him. Mr. Lowe's big, black hand ran up his arm, squeezing and pulling him forward enough that he was up-footed and fell forward into the big man's chest as he rose from his chair and pulled the kid into a bear hug. The strong smell of masculinity and cigar filled Michael's nose and he kind of went limp for but a moment until he regained his footing and thanked the big guy for the promotion and new position. Before the big guy let him go he noticed that the big guy had popped a huge woody and he was rubbing it against Michael, smiling down at him from his 6'6" height. Michael had admired the man's good looks, gloriously muscled masculine body and large hands and feet many times in the past, but now being so close to the big guy he too sprung a woody. Before Michael returned to his desk, just off to the side and facing Mr. Lowe's huge desk, the big guy said, "Michael, you and me are going to get along just fine boy!" He winked at Michael, adjusted his basket with one hand and sat back down in his large leather chair to light up another Cigarillo. The rest of the day until quitting time, Sarge spent time getting Michael up to speed handling the memos, transcripts and other correspondence he would be dealing with in his new position as personal secretary to Mr. Lowe.

By the end of the day, Michael was up to his ears in new tasks he only had briefly been introduced to by Sarge, whom had previously had this position. Come to find out, Sarge was also being promoted to the position as head personnel Sergeant with a rank of Master Sergeant. Three other guys in personnel received promotions. After supper Michael rushed to Sarge's door and knocked. Sarge was waiting, nude with a big smile on his face as he kicked the door shut, lifted Michael up into his arms and kissed him. He carried Michael to his bed, laid him out and crawled up on top of him and devoured the youngin with his huge thick lips. Michael was on fire and ready for his dessert by the time Sarge nibbled on his nipples and licked his still tender bottom. Sarge too was hot to trot, and was greasing up Michael's rosebud and working fingers into him before long. Michael was responding as Sarge expected, moaning and accepting what ever pain was involved to please his man. Before long Sarge had Mike on his back with his legs up over his shoulders feeding his black python into the boy's dilated pussy. Slowly Michael consumed it all as it snaked down into his excited womb. Once Sarge brazed the magic button, Michael was turned on to what ever his man wanted to deliver. Sarge was easy on the little guy and fucked him with total concern for not just his own pleasure, but that of Michael's also. With love and devotion could be described as how the two made love that evening – slowly, and with self control so as not to make Michael's pussy lips any sorer than necessary to accomplish what they both wanted from each other. Sarge brought them both to a loving orgasm, kissing, fondling and nipping at the boy's neck and ears as they both succumbed to their mutual pleasures. Sarge lowered Michael's legs down on the bed as he softened and slid slowly from the sphincter. He climbed up over the boy and fed his deflating cock into Mike's mouth for cleanup, then rolled him over on his tummy, spread his moons and ate out his own juices, licking, sucking, slurping and devouring until Mike was also clean and tidy.

Sarge hopped off the bed, grabbed the ointment and administered it cautiously to the swollen membrane, working some up inside to sooth him up there as well. They lay together watching the small TV mounted on the wall until it got dark. About 2300 hour they awoke. They grabbed towels and headed for the shower where Michael dropped to his knees under the warm spray of the showerhead and sucked Sarge until he dropped yet another tasty load of jizz into his new white lover-boy's throat. He let Michael sleep with him until he woke at around 0230 hours, put another layer of ointment on his rosebud and sent him off to his own bed.

The following two days went as well as could be expected with Michael learning his new job. He did notice from his desk that Mr. Lowe was constantly watching him. Every time Michael would look his way the big man would smile swivel his chair sideway so he was faced directly at Michael and adjust his equipment watching Michael's eyes drop to his crotch in total amazement. Of course, where Michael's desk was located in relation to the placement of Mr. Lowe's desk, no one else in the office but Michael could see what the big guy was doing when he got Michael's attention. By Thursday, Mr. Lowe had his pants open and his huge black Anaconda laying dormant down over his huge eggs and against the leather material of his oversized executive chair, teasing Michael with his entire package. Michael was flabbergasted, a bit upset, but what could he do but try to either ignore the man's bold exhibitionism, which might piss the big guy off and cause him to loose his current standing with the big boss man, or just sit back and enjoy the show and see where and what developed. In reality, Michael could not help but feast his eyes on the huge black beauty.

Each night Michael was anxiously running to Sarge to get loved. After the third day, Michael was no longer swollen and sore after Sarge took his pleasures inside his honey pot. By Friday night Michael was begging for some rougher treatment to his boy-pussy, especially after watching Mr. Lowe put on a show for him the very afternoon he got his promotion and new job and every day since then. That Friday night Michael finally told Sarge about the antics Mr. Lowe was performing each day, plus the fact that today he had actually jacked himself up to full glory and shook it at Michael from behind his desk seated in his chair.

Sarge let out a huge laugh and said, "That dirty old mother-fucker is still up to his same old dirty tricks, but it is to be expected babe. How do you think we get our promotions working for him? They didn't come without a cost babe. Yea, he knows about us and will be hitting on you before much longer too. What do you think I had to put up with for over two years now boy? The guy is married with three almost grown kids, pushing 50, bisexual and will fuck anything with a warm hole. You will just have to play along like most of us in the department have had to do to keep the old guy happy." He's mostly an exhibitionist, but I've had to suck him off quite a few times to keep him liking me enough to recommend me for promotions. Poor old Sergeant Beamer in payroll has had to let the old man fuck him in the storage room regularly since he was promoted to Staff Sergeant. Just go along with him, try to keep cool about it and everything will work out fine! You understand Babe?"

Michael muttered, "Yes Sarge! I can't believe what he carries between his legs Sarge. How big is that thing anyway?"

"Well, I couldn't get it down myself, but Beamer said he measured it and it was just a fraction over 14 inches long and as big around as a beer can. No wonder I couldn't get the mother-fucker down my throat. He soon learned I was strictly a TOP guy myself when I kept scraping my teeth on his dick until he stopped chasing after my ass and I flat out told him I'd share my pussy-boys with him, but to lay off thinking he was going to make my ass his pincushion. Everything's been great since that day, except he now expects to share my boys whenever the urge befalls him, which isn't too often as I'm sure he is getting ass at home with his beautiful wife. One of these days soon he will be asking you to stay late at the office, or come back after supper to do a special project he is working on. Let that be your cue to be nice and clean for the old guy and just go along with him if you don't want to get stuck in some shitty job like Robins, McClousky, Blake and Richards. They wouldn't put out and see where they are."

"Well, I guess I'll have to do what I have to do Sarge. If I can handle you, I certainly can handle him. He doesn't seem any bigger around than your cock; you're as big around as a beer can too. I'll just have to take another few inches in length. I'll start carrying a magnum rubber and a small tube of KY in my jacket pocket for when the day arrives that I have to service the old guy. Actually he isn't too bad to look at Sarge, all muscled up and in shape like he is. I just hate the smell of those damn Cigarillos he smokes though. He reeks of them. I just hope he doesn't want to kiss me – yuck! Sarge, thanks for being up front with me! Now I know what to expect and can be prepared for his advances. You're a real keeper Sarge and I really like being your boy."

Sarge said, "Hell Babe, it is Friday night, let's get stoned and maybe have a shot of Wild Turkey too before Rolf gets here. Tomorrow the three of us are going into Seattle so you can meet a couple of our friends – Lenny, one of my ex pussy-boys from a couple of years ago, and his Top Jaraald that runs a big stable of honeys at a brothel, both boys and girls of all ages. Jaraald has been a friend for years, knew him when I was growing up in Philly. Wait until you see the dude. He is what even I have to say is awesome and runs a first class business supplying the upper class male citizens of Seattle with any kind of services they may need for the right price."

A Boner Book

CHAPTER FOUR

"Sarge, those Valium pills you been giving me all week really have me screwed up big time. I'm spaced out, floating in a bizarre lustful dreamland most of the time thinking of you and Rolf – you are fucking me and Rolf has those beautiful big lips kissing me all over. I'm so turned on to you both I can't concentrate on anything else. Earlier today when Mr. Lowe was exposing himself to me, I couldn't keep my eyes off his big black boa. I think I even blew a few kisses at it I got so turned on. I'm not sure if even that was a dream or reality. I don't like this feeling of being out of control of my own actions and the emotions I keep having. I don't want to take any more of those damn pills. Half the time I don't know if what is being said is a dream or reality. For example, you know, Sunday night I had a strange dream where Rolf was telling you a story about this Lenny and Jaraald that you just said we were going to visit in Seattle tomorrow, because in the dream Rolf was telling you about a transsexual called Lenny that use to be one of your boys. I've been thinking all week about what Rolf told you about this girly boy Lenny and his black boyfriend Jaraald. The whole thing was too uncanny to possibly be true. It was like a dream; however, I'm still not sure if what I heard is what he really said to you, especially now that you say you and Rolf are going to take me to visit Lenny and Jaraald in Seattle tomorrow. In the dream Rolf also said that when Lenny was discharged from the service, you two took him to Seattle and sold him to Jaraald to turn into one of his male prostitutes in a brothel he operates. Now, isn't that one peculiar and wacky dream? You and Rolf wouldn't sell someone to a house of prostitution. Tell me it was just a bizarre dream Sarge."

"Well Babe, that wasn't a dream – it really happened! It was the best thing we could do for Lenny, actually for all of us at the time. He was becoming a real embarrassment, a real drain on all of us trying to keep him sexually satisfied and safe from real harm. He got so he wouldn't take orders and we never knew who was fucking him on the side. He had turned into a total slut and nymphomaniac a few months before his discharge date arrived. He liked the real rough stuff and was sneaking off at night to Tacoma and hitting the ghettos and the straight all black bars picking up rough trade, dock workers, any guys that would knock him around and use him for their pleasure. Unfortunately, they would get real violent and beat the shit out of him for being a fucking honky faggot after they got their rocks off. He would return back to the base after getting gang banged all bruised, fucked up on drugs, bleeding and hurting. He even had a couple of cracked ribs and a broken nose once. He just couldn't be trusted, so we had no choice but to take his pussy ass to Jaraald to put to work full time after his 18 months in the military ended and he was discharged. We did him a big favor doing that too, as we knew Jaraald could keep him satisfied sexually, busy and out of trouble. He would probably be six foot under now had we not found him a safe place to do his thing. The fact that Jaraald paid us for bringing him another male whore just made it better. Where do you think I would ever get enough money saved up to buy that new van a couple of years ago I now have?"

"So it wasn't a dream after all! Well Sarge, I want you to know that I have absolutely no intention of ever allowing you guys to start me on those hormone and estrogen shots to give me boobs like Rolf suggested and wants you to do to me, if that part was true too. No way! I may be getting more effeminate, acquiring a taste for sucking cock and like getting my ass fucked by your big black dicks, but I'm still a guy and won't submit to being turned into a transvestite or a transsexual with boobs, and certainly not a street whore for you two, this Jaraald, or anyone else. You and Rolf best not even go there with further ideas of changing me into a girl or half girl with or without a dick! I'll just find me another couple of boyfriends that like me the way I am thank you!"

"Oh you think so do you? Just listen to you giving me orders! You'll do exactly what this nigger tells you to do to get this big black dick shooting hot jizz down your throat and up that boy-pussy. I own your sweet cracker ass now Bitch. The minute I popped your cherry, opened you up and turned you on to my big black dick, you were mine. I virtually turned your boring life around, changed it forever for the better. You're getting exactly what you want from Rolf and me girl. You're still learning to enjoy all the real pleasures that a big nigger dick can deliver. The fact is, you are our white pussy-boy and cock-sucking bitch already and you love how Rolf and I make you feel. You keep coming back for more already. You will never be able to ignore the cravings you're having for our black muscled bodies, the taste and smell of us, and especially our big juicy dicks filling you with Nigger Jizz. There's no denying who and what you are now Bitch. Just surrender yourself to the fact that your sexual cravings have blossomed into a full time worship of our big black, juicy nigger dicks and it is just going to get stronger and stronger."

"I truly own your ass now, so if I decide to give you drugs that will give you boobs and big sensitive nipples, that's exactly what is going to happen to you Babe!" He paused a moment, opened his pants and flopped out his huge flaccid dick and balls and let them hang out so Michael had full view of his equipment. He grabbed Michael by the hair and pushed him to the floor on his knees and rubbed his cock and balls all over the kids face as he hardened and pre-cum started oozing from under his foreskin covering the boy's face, eyelids, and lips. When Michael tried to grab it and put it between his lips, Sarge stepped back and took it away from him watching his eyes follow the huge juicy cock and long meaty danglers get placed back inside Sarge's trousers, covered up and out of sight. Michael looked up into Sarge's eyes with a longing in his eyes, they glazed over and tears formed and dripped down his cheeks.

Sarge continued, "What I've given you can be taken away just that quick Bitch! I'm only going to tell you this once, so open your ears, stop your sniffling and pay attention to what I have to say. Never disobey me when I give you an order. Don't make me hurt you to get you to obey me, as I can be one mean mother-fucking nigger when my bitch starts giving me shit, telling me what they want in our relationship and putting demands on me before they will submit to my sexual appetite. I'm your superior, your dominant Alpha male and assertive Master. Your entire existence and future is under my total control as my submissive. I give the orders and decide what's best for you – you will learn to follow them without hesitation, without sass, backtalk or looks of disapproval or disgust. Once you learn this well, you will be where you need to be to be happy and contented; fight me and I'll cut you off and discipline you until you learn your place is at my feet worshiping my nigger dick and balls, as I am your Master and your new found life force. Now get those Valium pills out of my locker, as they seem to be doing exactly what I want them to do. In fact, I am going to double up on them for awhile after listening to you spout off, thinking you can put demands on my plans for your future. Will you ever learn – and here I thought we were past the defiant stage in your development! How dare you to ever question my position as your Dominant TOP, your Master and Nigger Daddy ever again! A double dose of Valium should keep you calm and complacent in nana land until you learn your new position in life well. Now get the fuckin Valium pills out of my locker Bitch."

Sarge bitch slapped Michael's face a couple of times when he hesitated and glared back at Sarge and stood there with a look of defiance in his eyes, but he knew better than to say a single word more after the lecture. Sarge shouted, "Now get nude and get the fucking Valium capsules out of my locker bitch like a good Bitch and bring them to me before I really loose my temper and put some real marks on that pretty girlie body where they won't show, but hurt real bad for a few days as a constant reminder of what you are and who turned your life around and now brings you pleasure beyond your wildest dreams. I am the man and your Master now Bitch. In fact, I want you to call me MASTER SARGE from now on, since I am now a Master Sergeant, but to you it will always mean MASTER, as in OWNER. Do you understand what I just told you Bitch?"

The tears flowed from Michael's eyes as he looked at Sarge who was holding him by both shoulders and looking down into his glazed over eyes just inches from his face. "YES, MASTER SARGE!" Michael turned and headed to Sarge's locker, rubbing his jaw. He returned with the capsules and handed them to Axel.

"Get the bottled water too!" Michael turned and retrieved the water from the top of the desk and returned to Sarge's side, still crying and softly rubbing his sore jaw. Sarge pushed two pills into the kid's mouth. He watched Michael swallow them with a couple of swigs of water, ran a finger around inside his mouth to make sure he had swallowed them both and said, "That's better girl, now tell me who I am and that you are sorry you upset me and won't act up and put demands like that again on me or hesitate when I give you an order."

"I'm sorry Master Sarge! I know I am your Bitch and I'll try to be better and not put demands on you."

"That better Baby! Now get out of those cloths; I'm horny and need to drop a load down your throat, maybe get some of that pretty white pussy ass too. You learn to take care of your Master's needs and I will protect and take care of keeping you sexually satisfied and happy too after you give me pleasure. Any questions Bitch?"

"No Master Sarge, except I don't like being called a Bitch, Cunt or..." Sarge cut off Mike's conversation before he could expand or add anything more to his sentence.

"SHUT THE FUCK UP MOTORMOUTH! No more small talk or whining. I don't want to hear another word out of you unless I ask you a question for now. UNDERSTOOD! I call em how I see em and right now you are definitely being a BITCH and a FIRST CLASS CUNT! I hear the defiance in your voice even yet, and it HAS TO GO!" He Bitch-Slapped Mike again, popped him hard on the ass a couple of times and knocked him across the room with his big booted foot to crash against his metal locker before he continued. "NOW GET MOVING BITCH!" Michael undressed, folded his clothing and placed them on a chair, then turned, returned to Sarge's side and started to undress him, hanging his clothing properly in his locker as he had been trained, sniffing at the wonderful scent filling the air around Sarge's sweaty nude body as it became fully exposed. Eventually Michael could hold back no longer and just buried his nose in the big guy's chest and rubbed it back and forth in the tight little circles of moist kinky hair that covered his chest and abdomen, ending up lifting Sarge's one arm and burying his nostrils in the longer coarse damp hair of his armpit. The aroma of sweat and male pheromones acted as an aphrodisiac to Michael's nervous system. Sarge allowed him to sniff, lick and suck in his pits for awhile, then pulled away and pushed down on

over his tongue and taste receptors. As Sarge relaxed and his dick slowly went flaccid, he pulled out of the boy's mouth.

"Clean me up with your tongue girl. Pull the skin back and clean the head and glands up good too. Don't forget what tricked down into my pubes and on to my hangers. Then get down there and lick up that mess you let spill on the clean tile floor." Sarge was sitting at his desk rolling joints when Michael rose from his hands and knees from cleaning up the floor. He stood behind Sarge and laid his head on his shoulder and kissed Sarge on the neck. Sarge pushed him away with a look of disgust on his face.

"Damn girl, you stink, smell like piss and cum. Put on your pants and go take a shower and brush your teeth and gargle with something. Take one of those containers of Fleet Enema in the bottom of my locker too and clean yourself out inside real good. Bro Rolf will be here before long and you know how he likes to kiss and make out with you with those big nigger lips and eat your pussy with that magic tongue of his. I remember you saying he has the biggest lips and was the best kisser, but with that breath of yours right now, I doubt he would touch your mouth with his suction cup wall hangers. Get moving and get back here quickly. I want you squeaky clean and all lubed up when you return. In fact I want that pussy kept nice and clean, lubed and ready for action 24/7 from now on girl."

While Michael was gone Rolf arrived and they discussed Lenny's big breasts and nipples. Sarge told Rolf about Michael's being awake and overhearing the entire conversation when they thought he was asleep. He told Rolf that Michael must have heard everything, even the part about Jaraald's plans on taking Lenny to Mexico to perform a partial Penectomy of his genitalia.

A half hour had passed and Michael was all squeaky clean, had lubed himself well, changed into a pair of sexy long nylon running shorts, a silky-smooth tee to match, and of course, his new leather sandals. He was walking down the hallway to return to Sarge's room when he passed an open doorway. He automatically paused and gazed into the room and saw a huge Confederate Flag hanging over the far windowed wall just before the room went completely dark. Suddenly a figure rushed out of the dark, grabbed him and pulled him into the pitch dark room into the arms of another guy that held him in place. It all happened in an instant. Coming from the well lit corridor, he was temporarily blinded and unable to see either assailant clearly. The door slammed shut and the familiar sound of a deadbolt being engaged registered. Total darkness was all Michael experienced other than the feel of arms holding him as a blindfold was placed over his eyes. A deep voice with a heavy southern drawl bellowed in the darkness just inches from his face.

"You best remain quiet, not a peep out of your nigger loving lips. It's despicable what you been doing with those niggers, Boy. I see you running every night to be with that black ass nigger and his buddy. Well, you're going to find out what we do with white trash that let the nigger bucks have their way with them in the south. You're a disgrace to the human race boy, and you best mend your ways." They pulled Michael's tee shirt off, dropped his drawers and removed his sandals, leaving him completely nude. The deep southern voice continued, "Light the candles at the cross boys." Michael was gut punched, fell forward and was caught by another, rotated 190 degrees and sent headlong into another barrage of punches to the gut, chest and to the head, knocking him out. When Michael came to, he was spread eagle sprawled on the floor on his knees and one guy was holding his face waiting for him to come around. The minute he showed signs of life the guy had him by the ears face fucking him. Someone else was already ramming what felt like a telephone pole size cock up his ass. He kept slipping in and out of consciousness as he was molested and called white trash, nigger lover, fucking queer and pussy-boy.

Michael was not sure, but figured at least three guys, maybe four screwed him before they propped him up in a chair and began a ritual of chanting and humming that had to be right from some Ku Klux Klan ceremonial handbook. He could tell by the feel that they were drawing or writing on his body with what felt like stiff bristled brushes and felt pens. What ever it was it was they were painting on him, it was still warm and smelled like rotting road kill. When they were finished they punched him out again. He awoke nude, laying in his bunk in his cubical, his clothing and sandals in a pile at his side and Sarge and Rolf nursing him back to consciousness with a damp washcloth on his forehead and face.

Sarge whispered, "When you were gone for an hour, Rolf and I started looking for you Babe. We looked here first, but you weren't here in your cubicle, the showers or bathroom; so we separated and started looking other places. You've been gone for just under two hours now. By the look of you, those mother-fucking southern boys have been fucking with you with their Klan shit. I've just about had it with those fuckers and their sick southern christen values, the confederate flags they all display in their lockers and rooms, and the hatred they have for blacks, Jews and any other minorities. It turns my stomach. I know who their ringleader is and he and I are going to have a showdown now that I am a Master Sergeant like him. They have done this to others, even Lenny a few years back, but the mother-fucker out ranked me and I could have been court marshaled if I tangled with him. His day has come Babe! I'm going to fuck him up real good for doing this to you Baby - not today, but soon. I'll just wait until he thinks we don't know who he and his group are, then strike and fuck him up real proper, end with fucking his Klan ass until he bleeds and cries for mercy. Just look at the sick shit they drew and wrote all over your body in what looks and smells like rotten chicken blood. They even drew a big Nazi Swastika on your back and a red target around your pussy hole with a red marker pen. They are really sick fuckers preaching their hatred and bigotry!"

Rolf added, "Let's get Mike in the showers and clean him up Sarge before this shit dries and sets up as a permanent stain on his smooth white skin. Damn that blood stinks they put on him; it makes me want to puke. Someone in here had to have seen them when they brought him back to his cubicle. They are probably afraid to say anything knowing that they would be punished too. There wasn't a sole in sight when we got back in here and found him, but there were guys everywhere when we first looked for him here earlier."

Sarge carried Michael to his room as Rolf gathered his shorts, tee and sandals and followed. Once the two moved Michael to the bathroom and in the shower cleaning him up, they could see the many bruises that were forming and the reddened anus that was still dilated and puffy, proof that he had been severely raped by the group of southern rebels. When they got Michael back to Sarge's room the big guy put liniment on his cuts, bruises and worked a good amount over his anus and up into his anal cavity feeling for any tearing or damage. Finding none, Sarge turned back his bed and put Michael in and covered him up, gave him a kiss and told him to rest and go to sleep. Rolf followed by leaning over and putting his lips to Michael's and giving him a long sensuous kiss. Michael quickly dropped off to sleep.

Sarge and Rolf smoked a couple of joints and sucked up Wild Turkey playing cards far into the night. Occasionally one or the other would set their cards down on the desk, rise to their feet and walk over and check on Michael when he would moan or stir in his sleep, stroking the boy's blond hair and sniffing at the clean smell of Irish Spring soap before kissing him on the forehead and returning to the cards. By 0200 hour they were both stoned and feeling no pain. Neither had bothered to dress after they came from the showers and bedded Michael for the night. They even removed the damp towels they had around their waists the minute they entered Sarge's room. With both the marijuana and the Wild Turkey in their system, they both periodically were sporting semi's and occasionally stroking themselves as they tossed cards and passed money back and forth into their individual piles of mostly dimes, nickels, quarters and single greenbacks.

They both looked at each other in astonishment as there was a light tapping on the door. Sarge said, "Now who the fuck could that be, it's after 0200 hour and I'm not expecting anyone this late?"

CHAPTER FIVE

Rolf said, "It might be Jamie Whiteman, the new kid in communications that arrived Monday right out of electronics school back east. The Lieutenant assigned him to me to help test, repair and calibrate all our electronic equipment. He's a real cutie with bright red hair, green eyes and covered with freckles all over his clear white skin. Wait until you see the bubble ass on him. Every time I'm around him I spring a boner; so today I put on a little show for him as we worked alone together in the storeroom. Sure enough, he couldn't keep his eyes off me, staring at me, especially my crotch with dreamy eyes. I asked him if he liked what he was looking at and he blushed and turned a bright shade of red. He finally mustered his composure and said he liked my big sexy lips. I grabbed my crotch, gathered the material of my fatigues around my equipment so he could see the outline of my dick clearly. I shook it at him until I had a full blown woody. He was instantly mesmerized, eyes fixed on my crotch as he unconsciously began to lick his lips. I told him if he was interested in having a taste and taking a test ride to come by my room later and I'd work him into my busy schedule. His blush turned to a big dimpled smile as he continued to stare at my dick. He started to say something, but backed off and didn't answer because the door opened and two guys stepped into the storeroom."

Rolf continued, "Before Jamie left after work, I told him I would be expecting him later in my room if he was still interested in getting down and dirty with my black juicer. Jamie smiled and said that would work for him, but it might be late when he returned back from Tacoma this evening, wiggled his bubble butt at me as he left. I'm convinced the kid is no virgin and either already has been with black guys or eager to get a taste of some black meat. Before I came over here to your room, I left a note on my door telling him I was in your room and to come around no matter how late. Maybe it's Jamie now! Don't get up Sarge, I'll get the door! It has to be him!"

As Rolf opened the door slowly, there stood this young good looking redheaded kid covered in freckles wearing a light green tee shirt, a pair of tan pleated slacks, brown belt and a pair of brown penny loafers. He smiled at Rolf, looked further into the dimly lit room but really couldn't see anything.

Jamie looked back at Rolf and the first words out of his mouth were, "I'm sorry I couldn't get back sooner Rolf, but I just got back from Tacoma and hoped you would still be up. When I read the note you left for me on your door I was relieved. I've been looking forward to this moment all evening." He looked up and down Rolf's nude body and zeroed in eyeing the big boner standing straight up against Rolf's stomach drooling pre-cum from the exposed lighter purple mushroom head down the darker shaft into the nest of long kinky black pubes. He snickered and said, "Well, I see you're still up alright Rolf; so are you going to invite me in big guy?"

Rolf pulled him into the room and bolted the door giving him a strong enough tug it lurched him into the half darkened room and he stumbled over Sarge's big feet seated in a chair smiling, obviously pleased with the kid's appearance and the play on words. Jamie caught himself from falling quickly, turned and Rolf was promptly at his side with his hand on the young boy's shoulder turning him back toward Sarge.

Rolf said, "Jamie, this is my best friend and buddy Master Sergeant Axel Wood, but we call him Sarge, and that's Specialist Fourth Class Michael Hunt there asleep, so talk quietly so as not to awaken him.

Sarge is training him to be his submissive Pussy-Boy. Michael has had a troublesome evening and needs his beauty sleep. Give me a little sugar and show me how you like my nigger lips sucking on your pretty pinks. He grabbed Jamie around the waist, held him firmly to his nude body and began to suck face, running his hands up under Jamie's tee shirt and lifted it up and off over his head. He tossed it in his pile of clothing in the corner and continued kissing as he squeezed the boy's nipples, rolling them between his fingers until they stood hard and erect. The boy began to moan with pleasure. He obviously liked his nipples worked.

Sarge was hard and stroking himself as he rose from his chair and pulled the two toward him. He wrapped one arm around the boy's waist from the rear and sniffed at the bright red-hair, putting his lips to the boy's ear and nibbling as he undid his belt, the button on his slacks and lowered the zipper. Sarge pushed his hand down between boxers and bare ass cheeks, rubbing the rough palm of his other hand over the two globes of soft skin, letting his long fingers separate and massage between the two bubble melons until the boy was rotating his hips and pushing back against the big paw moaning even more intently. Sarge gradually lowered the boy's slacks and boxers together until they fell around his loafers.

Jamie had his hand around Rolf's cock spreading the pre-cum along the hard shaft as the kid stepped out of his loafers and pulled his bare feet from his slacks and boxers, one foot at a time with Sarge's help, and kicked them into the pile of discarded clothing. Sarge removed his hand and wedged his hard cock shaft between the smooth cheeks and rubbed his dick up and down between the soft warm moons as copious amounts of pre-cum gathered in the channel making a slippery slick that worked down and covered the boy's pinkish rosebud. Sarge returned his hand in next to his dripping cock gathering more pre-cum on his fingers. He was soon working his slick fingers into the receptive rosebud until it burst into full bloom and pulsated, allowing four huge black digits, one at a time, to enter and finger fuck the anal canal until the boy's buns were pounding back trying to amputate the four troopers at the third knuckle. Sarge located and massaged the little hard walnut up inside until Jamie was as a rag doll in his arms and seriously pumping his buns back over the digits softly moaning, "Please! Oh please fuck me Rolf! I have wanted you inside me all week and really need you to feeding my hungry ass now!"

Sarge said, "Rolf he's all dilated, slick and hot to trot - ready for you buddy." He pushed his knees into the back of the Jamie's knees lowering him into the doggie position. Rolf traded positions with Sarge and slid right into the boy-pussy that had obviously been into the submissive jockey circuit for some time and was use to being rode fast, long and hard. Jamie was soon moaning, "Harder Rolf – fuck me like you love me! Make me your Bitch!" Sarge had to fill Jamie's mouth with his dick to keep him from screaming like a banshee princess in a fit of lustful bliss as Rolf gave him exactly what he was wanting. Sarge held him by the ears and pumped all his length down his throat while Rolf rode the boy's pussy all the way home, balls slapping against the firm bubble buns. Rolf tried to hold off his climax, but found it impossible with the steady milking action of the boy's talented pussy, depositing a massive load of sweet tasting jizz into the wild banshee's well trained, sizzling and hungry love canal. Sarge pulled his massive erection from Jamie's mouth as Rolf pulled from the hungry pussy that was still trying to milk him again to full excitement.

Jamie begged, "Please don't stop Rolf – More! More! Please More!" Both Rolf and Sarge listened to the begging for but a moment, as Rolf motioned Sarge to slide in behind the little nymphomaniac and take over the breeding ritual of this first-class bitch in her heated frenzy of anal lust for more dick.

Sarge smiled at Rolf and said, "I'll take a ride on the Bitch now, fill her up and bring her to multiple orgasms. She obviously likes it rough Buddy Boy. I'll take you where you want to go Bitch!" They changed positions and Sarge buried his larger Boa into the hungry pussy. The boy's expert abilities turned Sarge into a wild stallion, pounding the young mare with everything he had, violently lurching, rotating and jabbing the little walnut along the pathway for as long as he could hold back without spewing. Jamie's pussy lips and internal milking manipulations kept the Sarge right on the edge of shooting a full load of jizz constantly. Sarge had run across hungry pussies in the past and was able to prolong his climax with strong concentration and experience. He successfully brought the boy off three times, spewing cunt juice down into Rolf's mouth that was on his back under the boy holding seven inches in his mouth receiving each of the tasty offerings. Finally, the fourth and final orgasm, a twitching and pulsating pussy-muscle milked Sarge to a massive climax. By this time Rolf was standing erect again, took the lead and slid right back into Jamie and dumped another load of baby makers into the receptive love canal, as Sarge filled the boy's mouth with his manhood and slowly dropped his second full load down into a very well trained cocksucker's throat and stomach. Jamie finally collapsed flat out on the 4x8 foot area rug Sarge had just recently purchased to cover the cold tiled floor, with Rolf laid over him full length nibbling on his neck, ears and shoulders. All three remained silent as they each came down from their lustful high and regained their normal vitals.

Rolf smiled at Sarge and commented, "The boy is a keeper Sarge, milked us both like a real pro. Someone obviously trained him well, but I now claim him as my Bitch, since you already have your own with Michael! Of course, I would rather share them both with you if it's all right Sarge! What say?"

Sarge answered, "Your damn well we will be sharing our Bitches Rolf! What a hungry pussy on this one; His cunt is a virtual milking machine once he gets those pussy lips around a hard dick. He is going to have to teach Michael how to do it A.S.A P.! WHOW! Talk about a well trained Pussy Bitch – Jamie definitely gets the blue ribbon from me!"

After Rolf had Jamie lick both Sarge and him clean, he and Jamie dressed and he pulled Jamie into his arms, gave him a big, sloppy wet kiss with his huge lips and said, "You're my Bitch now Jamie, so no more fucking around with other guys except Sarge without my OK! Now get your boxers on and come to my room down the hallway. I'll rock you to sleep in my arms Babe. They both left with Rolf holding Jamie by the shoulder and pushing him along, popping him on the ass lovingly, physically expressing his authority to the boy through this very dominant action.

Sarge was all sweaty from the workout, so ran to the showers down the hall with soap and a towel and was back in record time all squeaky clean. He crawled up behind Michael, spooning his toasty warm buns, sniffing his golden locks and neck until he too was sound asleep and cutting soft Z's. Morning came quickly as should have been expected; as it was well after 0400 hour when he finally was cuddled up behind Michael visiting the sandman.

Sarge and Michael slept right through the breakfast hours. They would have probably slept right through lunch also were it not for a tap on the door bringing Sarge slowly awake. With a rubbing of his eyes, Sarge answered the door to find Rolf and Jamie standing looking like they too had just crawled out of the sack and headed for the showers wearing only towels and carrying shaving kit and tooth brushes.

Rolf said, "Best get your buns up guys, lunch in twenty minutes. If you're as hungry as us you will get up and get going before the entire day is wasted. Jamie and I are headed to the showers and then to lunch. Join us and get this show on the road if you still plan on going to Seattle today."

Sarge wiped his eyes, looked at the clock and said, "Ok buddy, we will join you in the showers in a few minutes. Damn, I could eat a buffalo too, I'm so fucking hungry. We will talk about the Seattle trip over lunch!"

Forty minutes later the four were sitting in the mess hall eating when Rolf nudged Sarge and said, "Well if it isn't Master Sergeant Ross Wright and his southern rebel companions eyeing us from that table in the back of the room next to the officer's section.

Sarge answered, "Don't look around or stare at them guys or they will know we suspect it was them that molested Michael last night. Just pay them no mind or they will have their guard up and be expecting retaliation from us." Rolf had to explain to Jamie what had happened to Michael the previous evening.

When Rolf was finished explaining, Jamie said quietly, "That's odd, because MS Wright was real friendly to me Monday when I first arrived. In fact, I would swear he was coming on to me, and my Gaydar isn't often fooled. I was in the bathroom standing at the urinal taking a leak when he walked in and took the urinal right next to me. I didn't pay him much attention because he's so homely and pot marked; but when he pulled out that big long, fat dick of his, skinned it back and started pissing I couldn't help but stare at the huge monster in his hand. In fact, he didn't seem so fucking ugly after I got a good look at his equipment. He noticed me staring down at it too, and before he put it away he stepped back a bit, pulled the long skin back off the head and stroked it a few times until it was growing and getting hard. He looked into my eyes and smiled and then slowly put it away and went to the sink to wash his hands. He lingered there washing his glasses watching me wash and dry. He was still sporting a huge boner in his pants when I left. He definitely was going commando and it was really tenting his fatigues. I been around long enough to know the guy was coming on to me with his bold action. I even caught up with him on the way back to where we both work in the communications department and let him know that I was indeed interested in his friendship. He has been popping me on the ass all week when he knows no one is looking. Damn, I've never seen a white guy with equipment like he has. I guess it makes up for just how ugly he is otherwise."

Michael said, "Well the leader of the guys that raped me last night was huge alright. The rest were much smaller, in fact one was so short he had a hard time keeping it in me. Those little dicks can really do a lot of damage the way they stay real hard and work over the entrance to an asshole like the needle on a tattoo machine poking at an asshole rather than entering and delivering some pleasure. The guy with that little dick really hurt my asshole. Thank god he didn't last long or I wouldn't be able to walk today."

Sarge said, "Sorry Baby about what that little dick did to you, but yea, I figured as much about that mother-fucking ringleader MSgt. Ross Wright. That's great too, we can use Jamie when the time comes to lure him into our trap so we can do the same thing to him as he and his buddies did to Michael last night. Now don't any of you look at them as we leave, as that's what he is obviously watching for, indicating that we know it was him and his bigoted sick companions. I bet it really pisses him off to see Jamie with us today if he has an interest in him. Come on now, if we are going to Seattle we best get going." The four left and headed to the van that they loaded with a few items and their jackets before going to lunch.

Less then an hour later they were pulling up in front of a large elaborate wrought-iron gated entryway flanked on both sides with an eight foot ornate brick wall that seemed to surround the property. Sarge lowered his window and pushed a red button on the security box and a voice returned asking his identity. Moments later the gate slowly opened and they drove through into a lush park like setting of tall trees, blooming azaleas, camellias, rhododendrons and plantings under the shaded umbrella of the trees. Colorful flower beds filled the sunny spots along the boarders along the cobblestone driveway as it split and continued up the slight upslope property. A low boxwood hedge flanked the driveway all the way to a large parking area. They continued up until the house started to come into view. Both Michael and Jamie let out ahs as the full view of the huge tri-level English Tutor came into view, surrounded with beds of radiantly blooming flowers and colorful shrubbery. The house set on the top of a flat knoll in total grandeur with a matching five car detached garage off to the left.

Sarge pulled into a smaller parking area across the driveway and adjacent to the garage. They gathered the bags and made their way to the front covered entryway. The house was mostly covered with ornately sculptured brick with black metal framed delicately small-pained diamond beveled glass windows, typical of an English Tutor. The same sculptured brick formed a circular turret which housed the covered entryway. A solid ornate hand-tooled oak door, the upper half covered in beautiful stain glass and flanked by large stained glass fixed windows formed the main entrance. Two large matching carriage lamps hung from the high ceiling by chains. The place was grand.

Shortly after Sarge pressed the doorbell the huge oak door opened and an older white gentleman dressed in a butler's uniform stood erect looking at the group for a moment. The minute he recognized Axel and Rolf his business like manner changed and he put his hand out to Axel, smiled and said with a very British accent, "Good to see you and Master Rolf again Master Axel. Please come right in, as Miss Lenny told me in confidence you might be by today for a visit. If you will all be seated here for a moment I will jingle Miss Lenny of your arrival."

Sarge answered, "Thank you Bernard," and the four moved to the seating area in the center of the large circular space. The circular foyer was at least a sixty foot diameter with three long corridors leading off, one to the left wing, one to the right wing and the third leading straight ahead, ending in what looked like a large room with an expanse of clear beveled glass that looked out the back of the house. An open oak and wrought iron stairway circled up the inside oak and fancy brick walls of the circle, forming landings that circled the room at each of the other two stories. A beautiful fancy old black metal elevator sat opposite the base of the stairway. The open fancy metal framework leading all the way to the third floor landing, something we have all seen in old black and white movies filmed in England's mansions. The entire house was obviously furnished by a professional that knew how to mix antiques, ultra modern, traditional and contemporary style furnishings. Everything was massive and to scale for the large spaces. A huge ultra modern geometric area rug in the center of the room pulled everything together into a true Eclectic masterpiece of excellent design and beauty.

Bernard quickly returned and told them that both Master Jaraald and Miss Lenny were at the Cabana at poolside and wished them to join them immediately. They all rose and followed Bernard down the center corridor through what seems to be a large formal sitting area that opened through a alcove to the left into a large formal dining room. They were led straight through the sitting area, through large glass double doors on to a huge stone patio that was entirely surrounded with a low three foot wall constructed of the same stone material. The patio looked out over a formal meticulously maintained landscape mirroring the grounds on the way up the driveway, except close in and down three groups of five wide stone stairs, each separated with a wide landing until they reached another stone patio that surrounded a large tile pool and three large attached white canvas cabana buildings with the canvas rooflines resembling the sails of an old English Schooner like the roofline of the Denver, Colorado Airport Terminal of today.

As the five reached the cabana, Jaraald and Lenny rose from their shaded cushioned lounges. They both were totally nude and made no effort to cover themselves with the terry robes that were draped over the back of each of their lounges. Lenny ran toward them, breasts bouncing and arms extended and wrapped his arms around Sarge and laid a kiss on him, then turned and did the same to Rolf. Michael and Jamie looked at each other in total amazement for a moment, before Lenny broke away and led them to Jaraald.

Jaraald immediately wrapped his arms around Axel, gave him a big hug and put his hand out to Rolf and said, "Welcome Brothers! I see you both have adopted a couple of real beauties as usual."

Axel grabbed Michael around the waist and said, "Jaraald this is my new honey Michael Hunt," then pulled Jamie into his waist with his other arm and said, "and this is Jamie White, Rolf's new honey. Yea – they are both keepers. Michael has only been out for a week now, still getting Bitch trained. I have him on Valium since he is having a hard time getting use to the fact that I'm the Butch and he's the Bitch, though he's learned the basics quite quickly. Jamie, on the other hand, came to us already well trained and experienced in taking care of us big guys. He likes it long and rough and can milk a dick with his ass muscles better than any pussy-boy I have ever fucked. They both have mastered oral and anal, and are addicted to big black guys with big black juicy dicks. Now go give Jaraald some sugar girls!"

Jaraald pulled the two into his arms and gave them each a big kiss, squeezed their asses, and said, "Very nice! They are very nice looking, terrific bodies, and so very young and tender!" His huge endowment was already standing at half-mast and slightly dripping when he released the girls and said, "State your poison to Lenny and he and Roger will bring the drinks and goodies out to us in a jiffy while the four of you go into the change room and get nude so this dirty old nigger pervert can get a better look at your girls nude bodies. I could sure use them in 'The Stables' right now. I lost two of the best boys just this week. We have been looking for them, but I suspect they are long gone by now, as they had a thing for each other from what I'm told." Lenny took their orders and Axel and Rolf escorted the girls into the change room. Axel and Rolf undressed quickly and left their clothing in a heap on the floor instructing the girls to fold them and put them on the shelves proper like. The two guys rejoined Jaraald at the large round glass-top table.

Jamie and Michael took their sweet time undressing. While they dilly dallied undressing and doing as told, Jamie and Michael got into a private conversation about both Lenny and Jaraald. They both agreed that Jaraald was a real looker, built like a Black Adonis and hung like a Bull with huge loose dangling balls that could turn a girl's ass bright red as they slapped their pussy cheeks silly. As far as Miss Lenny, they thought he was very effeminate, pretty as a picture and liked the boobs and nipples. They wondered just how sensitive they were and wanted to ask him, but agreed his cock was so small they could understand why Jaraald wanted it removed and his balls sewed up inside him. There was no way he had enough cock and ball skin material to ever form enough of a female pussy to accommodate Jaraald's huge cock, and they haven't even seen it hard yet.

Jamie said, "I hope Jaraald gets that big dick hard so we can see just how big it gets. My mouth is drooling just looking at it laid over his balls flaccid. Did you watch it go to half-mast when he was holding us and fondling our buns! Wouldn't you like to have a go with him too Michael; he makes my pussy pucker and my heart thump?"

"Yea, but it probably isn't going to happen, as Sarge and Rolf would tan our hides if we do anything with him without their approval. We will just have to play it cool and hope they get frisky. I think the both of us are definitely a couple of white whores. Listening to us both; we are disgusting. We should be happy with what we already have. Must be the male in us yet! Yea, it is definitely a male trait!" They looked at each other and burst out into laughter.

Sarge must have heard them giggling and laughing, as he hollered, "Get your buns out here girls, the drinks are coming and Jaraald is anxious to check you out and maybe even take a test ride if you're lucky enough to qualify for his attention. Get a move on and get out here pronto and stand at attention next to your men where you belong. Don't make us come in there for your Cracker Ass Pussies."

The two were immediately at the side of their men standing at attention.

Roger and Miss Lenny arrived with the refreshments, Roger carrying the drinks on a large silver tray, followed by Lenny carrying an ornately carved box under one arm and another tray of finger food. Roger was an Asian guy, looked to be in his late 30's dressed like Bernard in a tailored butler's uniform. He sat the drinks on the table and asked Jaraald if there was anything more he wished. He was instructed to bring another round of the same in 15 minutes, sooner if he was summoned on the intercom. Roger answered with a prompt nod and returned to the house. Jamie handed the correct drinks to Jaraald, Axel and Rolf.

Sarge said, "At Ease girls and grab your drinks and sit down in a chair." Lenny joined the girls and the three sat quietly as the guys talked about mostly sports and pussy. As Roger was delivering the second round of drinks to them Jaraald told Roger that the four would be staying for dinner and spending the night as usual, so be sure and have the playroom tidy and the guest bedrooms prepared should they be used.

Jaraald turned to Axel and said, "We go back a long way Axel, clear back to when we grew up and went through grade and high school together in Philly. It seems like I've know and trusted you for a lifetime now Bro. I remember the first time we jacked-off together and when we screwed Penny Sanchez in the back of that garden shed. Those were the days Axel! I remember when that cracker queen Alan Spence begged us to fuck him when we were sophomores in high school. We couldn't get enough of that tight ass after that. He was a good eight years older than us, but when he got a good look and taste of our big dicks he was waiting for us every night in that van outside the pool hall so he could get his ass reamed and his mouth full of our big dicks. Before long we were searching for more crackers like him. It changed our lives forever Axel. Sure, we fucked the girls too, but we didn't like all the bull shit that went along with dating the girls and ending up not getting any. That's when we really started seeking out the gay boys in high school our own age and younger. It was great when we would get hold of a virgin and turn him into a bitch. The crazy thing was they kept coming back for more, no matter how rough we fucked them. They would be waiting for us at that old van of mine in the high school parking lot to be molested until they shot all over themselves. That pool hall storeroom saw a lot of action too for us. Those were the days!"

He hesitated for a few moments and then asked, "Axel, have you given anymore thought to joining me in the Seattle Pussy Business and getting off this idea of being a career military man and retiring with a measly two-bit pension after years of service under your belt and taking orders rather than giving them?" He didn't even wait for Axel to respond, as he went right on talking, "Hell Axel, I can't believe you would want to join up for another hitch doing what you are doing now when you could be living like a king like me and making millions having fun at the same time. What's up buddy?"

"You bet I been thinking about it a lot lately Jaraald. This hitch I'm on now will be all I need for full retirement, benefits and still have full access to the medical and retirement benefits the service offers retirees. I only have twelve and a half more months to go for full retirement Jaraald. After that, yes I am interested in joining you in your business. Michael has just about the same time left and he will be discharged. By then I hope to have him wanting to stay with me. I figure bringing him with me and eventually even getting him turned into a transsexual, a real woman. In fact, I want to start him on those shots or treatments to give him some boobs and big nipples like you've done with Lenny. You think if I started Michael on the treatments right away he could go a year before his boobs would be too large to hide if strapped down around the base?"

"Well, that's the first sensible thing I have heard you say about this for two years Axel. It takes at least 14 to18 months before his boobs would get too large to hide, but after about 6 to 8 months his nipples and breasts will be very sensitive and he will love to have them sucked on and played with. He will also loose body hair and start to widen in the hips and narrow at the waist. The best part is he will become more and more effeminate and horny, wanting and begging for your attention to his pussy, breast and nipples. He won't just ejaculate anymore, but truly have one anal orgasm after the other as you fuck him silly. He will love the new feeling he will experience. Just have him talk with Lenny about it and he will be begging us to get him started on the treatments."

What about the mood swings I've heard about Jaraald?

"Damn Bro., they have medications today to control the hot flashes and mood swings associated with taking Estrogen and other female enhancement drugs. In fact, it's kind of nice when Lenny gets all emotional and cries on my shoulder once in awhile. But the very best part is he looks and dresses as a woman and we can be seen together in public as a man and a woman. No one looks at us with that look of disgust anymore when we walk down the street hand in hand, except for the still bigoted that can't stand to see a black man with a white woman, especially if they are pretty like Lenny. Having Lenny the way he is now is one of the smartest things I ever did for us both. I can hardly wait until you and Michael join Lenny and me here in this big old mansion. I owe you and Rolf big time Axel for bringing Lenny to me a couple of years ago. Rolf, you will always be welcome to join us too, come the day you decide to leave the military and get into this profitable service business. I feel I can't do enough for you two buddies. I would have been starved for real love if Lenny hadn't come along to show me how real love between two people can make one's life worth living. Sure, we guys all fool around on the side when we see something that turns us on, but when you find someone that loves you and is always there for you, the love bug strikes deep and you always come home to your true love waiting for you at home."

He hesitated a moment and then continued, "That's where I am with Lenny guys, and next weekend we are going to fly down to Mexico to have his dick removed and his balls sewed up inside him so he will really feel like a real woman and my beautiful bride, as I plan on marrying him after the legal work is done to change his name and sex to make it legal. He won't have a real pussy, but he will still be able to ejaculate and have orgasms as I fuck his sweet ass like we do now. Even if he had a real female pussy, I would still prefer to fuck that nice tight hole and slap my danglers against his bubble buns. I can hardly wait for this all to be behind us so we can get hitched and maybe adopt a couple of kids. Guys, let's get really stoned and fucked up tonight and fuck the girls' silly to celebrate. What say?"

Axel and Rolf looked at each other and smiled; then Axel answered, "Works for us Jaraald. Let's do it!"

Jaraald opened the mystery box that Lenny had carried down earlier under his arm and sat on the table next to Jaraald. He opened the hinged lid said, "Help you to the goodies guys." Each of the guys pulled their girl into their lap and fed them an Ecstasy pill and lit up multiple joints and proceeded to get the girls ready for some serious action. Jaraald grabbed the intercom and instructed Roger to bring more drinks. A couple of hours later they were sitting at the dinner table stoned, drinking red wine, each shoveling down a large New York steak, baked potato and mixed green vegetables with slices of chocolate cake for dessert. They all retired to the play room on the second floor to enjoy the pleasures of rough sex with their three dominant black males.

By the time they had a few more high-octane alcoholic drinks, and smoked a few more joints the guys were all over the girls, knocking them around and tossing them back and forth in the air from one to the other. The girls were screaming and fighting for release afraid they would be dropped as they were tossed back and forth into the air to one another. The guys spanked their hot asses when they resisted their master's jabs, bites and rough horseplay, until their white buns were red and the girls became submissive to the antics.

Restraints were eventually put on the girls and they were passed from one guy to the other and face fucked until the guys decided it was time to pump their asses full of dick juices. The guys wore cock rings to keep from ejaculating prematurely and fucked the girls, constantly changing partners so each guy could thoroughly enjoy each hot pussy. The girls had many orgasms, until their balls were empty and all they could have were dry orgasms, one after the other as their pussies were ravaged into gaping holes. The guys eventually pulled off their cock-rings and covered the girls with their nigger jizz and they all crashed on the mats and fell asleep in the warm room. Jamie and Michael were the first to awaken. The two awakened Lenny and the three sneaked off to take showers and clean up before the guys missed them. When they returned the guys pretended they were asleep until the girls started sniffing their strong sweaty bodies. The guys grabbed them, seeing they were all clean and smelling good, they rubbed their sweat and masculine scent all over the girls again and made them drink their full load of strong piss.

By the time they were all sitting nude being served breakfast, they all stank to high heaven and the guys were feeding the girls large handfuls of scrambled eggs, mostly smearing it all over their faces, hair and bodies. They then licked the food from the bodies of the girls wrapping up the meal by laying the girls on the large oak table and standing over them jacking off, covering them with their warm cum, then forcing the girls to lick each other clean of the large deposits of the guy's warm juices.

CHAPTER SIX

"OK guys, time to hit the showers and let the girls clean us up; then we guys will go down to 'The Stables.' I need to check up on a few things and you can see the changes I've made in the place. Lenny, you give the girls the grand tour of the house then enjoy the pool or just sit around and trash us guys until we get back and show you three how to play some big boy games in and around the pool," Jaraald announced. He grabbed Lenny around the waist and headed back up to the playroom on the second floor followed by Axel and Michael, Rolf and Jamie. He opened a large door on the left side of the playroom and led them into a huge ultra modern bathroom, complete with a large glass enclosed, tiled and marble walk-in shower with multiple showerheads, a large Jacuzzi and steam room. He opened a panel and hit a few controls and the water started to pulsate from some of the heads in the shower while others shot a steady spray of steaming water. They all entered and the girls cleaned their men. When the girls had them clean, the guys stepped out and grabbed a towel from the racks and were drying as Jaraald changed the settings on the controls and three douche attachments dropped from a stainless steel panel, one below each shower head. Lenny took the lead and showed Michael and Jamie how to work the apparatus. The large drain system took care of their discharges. They showered and were soon dressed in nothing but white terrycloth robes and matching terrycloth slippers, as they joining the fully dressed guys on the first floor waiting in the large family room bellied up to the bar being served Bloody Maries by Roger the butler. The guys had one more drink with the girls playing grab ass with them until Jaraald hopped off his bar stool and addressed the guys.

"Ok, on your feet guys, we best go now before we get all horny and too plastered to take care of business. Lenny, you give Michael and Jamie a complete tour of the house and grounds and entertain them like a good hostess, but don't be going off the estate grounds in the Beamer today, especially if you're drinking." He turned to Roger and said, "We won't be back until about 3:00pm Roger, so the girls will be having lunch without us. Be sure and tell the cook we will be having dinner at 7:00pm sharp, the steak and lobster special will be fine with a big green salad. My guests will be staying over again until sometime tomorrow, Sunday." The guys gave each of their girls a big hug and kiss and they were off headed out for 'The Stables.'

Lenny, Michael and Jamie sat around a small cocktail table next to the bar and Roger continued to serve them Bloody Maries listening to Lenny tell of his exploits with guys over the years, both before and after he was discharged and left by Axel and Rolf with Jaraald. Wasn't long listening to Lenny's crazy days, as he referred to them, that Jamie started to inject some of the wild sexual experiences he had that got him turned on to the big well endowed guys, especially the blacks, that turned him into a total bottom for their lustful pleasures. The conversation eventually got around to Lenny's treatments and his feelings toward getting physically altered to please Jaraald. Lenny went into detail describing how he fell head over heals in love with Jaraald and wanted to do anything to make his man happy, starting with the treatments and eventually the shots and pills to give him boobs and big sensuous nipples. He told them they eventually became so sensitive that any stimulation on them got him so hot he just trembled inside and could actually ejaculate when Jaraald massaged and sucked on them. He said the pleasure he received from his breasts and nipples was totally new to him. He described it as almost as wonderful as getting Jaraald's big dick up inside him bringing him to multiple climaxes, the combination of both anal sex and nipple/breast play making him helplessly addicted to what ever Jaraald wanted to do with him.

Jamie boldly asked Lenny, "But how do you feel about having your cock removed and your balls sewed up inside you Lenny, isn't that a bit drastic, over the top, as my dick is what likes to get played with as I'm getting dick up the ass?"

Lenny answered, "At first I was terrified of the thought of loosing my dick, but then I realized that this last year of so it had become nothing more than something to pee through. Hell, since I have been on estrogen and the other hormones the doctor prescribes, it has shrunk up into just a little nubbins with little or no feelings of pleasure no matter how much I try to make it feel good like it use to when I masturbated. Sure, I'm not looking forward to the operation, but more out of fear of something going wrong with the operation being performed in Mexico than loosing my tiny wicker-bill. You heard Jaraald telling the guys why he wanted it removed. I love the big guy and will do what ever he wants to make him happy. He has learned to do a few things that are not of his nature to please me too, like giving me rounds of rough sex which I have always loved. He even has learned to talk dirty to me and is taking training from an S&M Master to give me what I crave so frequently. Yes, I am a pain freak and really get off on that shit. I can't help it, because when the pain gets intense, something in my brain kicks in and the pain turns to sheer pleasure. I admit it sounds a bit sick, but I absolutely crave it often, and Jaraald has learned, or is learning how to deal with it in a positive way through training with this S&M Master trainer that has been working with us for about six months now. Jaraald would have never in a million years done this without my constant begging and insistence, so you see he loves me and wants to make me happy too. I couldn't refuse him anything he asked me to do now. He is my Master and I am his love goddess and want to be his sex slave. He treats me like his queen until we get in the dungeon. There he is learning to give me what I crave from him. It was hard for him to hurt me at first, but he is learning how to do it without doing permanent damage with the trainer's assistance. The trainer Wilhelm Kuntz, a German and a real hunk, knows how to get all my bells and whistles activated. Jaraald is a quick learner and is starting to really turn me on with dirty talk, kink, rough sex and pain. I reach a level of pleasure I can't even put into words down in that dungeon he had built recently for us. It's our personal playroom. He and Wilhelm work me over together and I absolutely love what they do to me. Loosing my wicker-bill is a small price to pay for what I am getting from Jaraald in return. Come on now and I will give you the grand tour of the estate; plus, I have a special surprise for you during the tour of the grounds later." He rose, Jamie and Michael followed.

After touring the East and West Wings, portions that were still under extensive remodeling, Lenny gave them a tour into the basement of the East Wing that housed a full scale dungeon with all the S&M equipment and toys a Master and Slave could ever desire. Both Michael and Jamie stood in total awe as Lenny stopped at each major apparatus and went into detail describing what function it had, even demonstrating how it worked and how each turned him on in most unusual ways. Then they went out a side door that opened into the side yard and got onto a four person golf cart and were given a complete tour of the 20 acres of meticulously landscaped formal gardens. As they were finishing the tour of the gardens they came to a high spot in the terrain where they looked down upon an eight foot high hedged old English garden maze. It was huge looking down on it, probably each outside hedged wall of the rectangle structure 70 or 80 feet long. Lenny stopped the cart and pointed out two young gardeners that were working in the warm sun shirtless and in short cut-offs and leather work-boots wearing leather gloves. Lenny could see that both Michael and Jamie were impressed and staring at the two hot numbers manicuring the high hedge on ladders with electric clippers. They were still far enough away that they could talk freely without being heard by the workers.

Lenny said, "Jaraald lets me hire most of the garden crew guys since I speak Spanish, and those two beauties and a third that is probably inside the Maze trimming where we can't see him, I hired. I trained them from day one to play around big time with me, give me what Jaraald wasn't at the time. They are my surprise for us this morning! Are you interested in playing hide and seek in the maze with them this morning girls? Two are actually Cuban and the one inside is a Chicano/Mexican. All three fuck like bandits, are uncircumcised and hung like bulls. They will take your breath away once they get you cornered in the Maze with nowhere to hide or get away from them. They like to play rough and dirty hide and seek where they give us a five minute head-start so we can try to make it successfully to the center of the Maze without getting caught. Then they have to play by your rules. However, if they catch you alone at a dead end passage before you reach the gazebo in the center, you have to play by their rules and are in for a real treat of anything goes with them taking what they want and leaving you exhausted, rode hard and put away wet. I've taught them each to play rough like I like it, so expect the works if you give them any hint that rough and tumble is your pleasure. Well! Are you game girls, but you must never mention my games with them to the guys, especially Jaraald? He would fire them immediately and I would be in big do-do? I made sure the three were working the Maze today guessing you two would be interested in some extra fun and games not on the regular grounds tour itinerary. Oh yes! I hope you each like head cheese as much as I do, as they save it up for me at my request. They do get sweating and quite heady with that wonderful masculine smell and the taste of those little white speckled special treats are better than limburger cheese. If you don't like limburger cheese, just say NO, and they will cut to the chase and not make you eat the white stuff."

Jamie said, "Fuck YES and I love the stuff too," and Michael followed with "Works for me, Mmmm yea!"

Lenny continued, "Do either of you speak Spanish?"

They both answered, "No!"

"Great, it will be more fun for you two then, as they don't speak much English and they will have to communicate with body language with you two. You will love it girls!" He opened a compartment in the cart and handed both Jamie and Michael a small tube of lube and three large rubbers each. "Be sure and put a rubber on them girls, as these guys all fuck anything that moves or show the least bit of interest in pleasures of the body with them, male or female. Now, I could give you a diagram of the Maze so you could find your way easily to the center without too much trouble, but it's more fun if you don't have a map and get caught in a trap or dead-end passage where you are cornered and at your pursuer's mercy. They each know not to hurt you girls or leave cuts, marks or bruises on you, but will try to scare you out of your mind, especially if you put up a good fight and force them to take charge and rape you. Get the picture?"

Jamie smiled and said, "We get the picture Lenny!" Michael nodded the affirmative.

Lenny smiled and said, "Ready girls! Here we go," and headed the golf cart toward the Maze. As they approached the two on the ladders, they looked over and began to smile and wave hoisting their loose, short cut-offs up partially exposing their balls and long flaccid cocks for viewing. By the time Lenny stopped the cart the girls had a birds-eye view up the ladders at the merchandise. Perched facing them down from the ladders, one shouted something in Spanish and the third young gardener exited the opening to the Maze and joined the other two. Both Michael and Jamie were amazed at the muscles and masculine beauty of the three as the two came down from the ladders and approached Lenny speaking their foreign tongue. Lenny communicated in Spanish with them for a moment, and then introduced them as Pedro, Santiago and Hidalgo, pointing to each as he said their names, then pointing to the girls and saying Jamie and Michael.

Lenny spoke to them again in rapid Spanish and they each listened as they smiled at the girls, groping their crotches and rubbing their stomachs. Their crotches expanded and their cocks jettisoned out from the leg holes of the short sheered cut-offs. The girls were all eyes checking out the three young stallions scoping them out. Pedro was obviously the Mexican, much shorter than Santiago and Hidalgo, but handsome with a body rippling with muscles and a handsome face with beautiful white teeth. He had hairy legs and arms, but his abdomen was relatively hairless except for a treasure trail of black hair funning down the center of his chest, then from his navel to the top of his shorts. Santiago and Hidalgo on the other hand were taller and larger guys, bulging with muscles, eight pack abs and hairy chests, legs and arms. They had the good looks of so many mixed breed Cubans. Their expanding cocks were a light shade of black and of course uncircumcised and the heads that gradually peeped out were of a lighter shade of reddish purple. Pedro had the shorter cock, but it had the circumference of a beer can. Hidalgo had to exceed 10 inches in length, but Santiago was at least 12 inches or more with the width of a beer can also. There was no hiding what they were packing as they stood fondling themselves as the girls drooled. A few more exchanges of Spanish dialog between Lenny and the guys and Lenny turned to Jamie and Michael and opened his short robe and instructed the girls to do the same. He bounced his boobs at the boys. Their eyes rolled and their cocks throbbed and began to drool and bubble cock-snot.

Lenny instructed, "Give the guys a good look at your bodies girls and let them decide which one of us they each are going to pursue. Bend over and spread your buns so they can see it all girls. Don't be bashful at a time like this. The hotter we get them, the better they will perform. That's it! Now wiggle your caboose at them and follow me. I'll take the left passage, Jamie you take the center passageway and Michael you take the right." He told the guys in Spanish which pathway they each would be taking and grabbed the girls and led them through the entranceway and they each went their separate direction working their way between the tall sculptured walls of the dense green hedge. The girls were separated now and making headway, making choices at each junction to go left or right, proceeding through the maze, sometimes coming to a dead-end and having to retrace their steps to the last junction and choose another route. Lenny of course, knew the way to the center and was making great progress; however, both Michael and Jamie were at a loss as to what direction to go time and time again, until eventually the five minute head start had well passed and they were each hopelessly lost and soon were each up against a dead-end cubicle sporting a comfortable chase lounge big enough to accommodate two grown adults. They each realized it was the end of the road for them as they each reclined on the lounge and buttered up their honey pots and waited, wondering which one of the young studs would be in pursuit and lusting for their prize.

Jamie was the first to receive his pursuer. Santiago entered the cubical nude and in full pursuit, 12 inches of manhood bouncing and his ball sacks bouncing against his inner thighs. He pounced on Jamie, spread out on the chase lounge, squirming and rubbing his sweaty body all over her. He threw a leg up over Jamie, sitting on her chest and fed his massive manhood between Jamie's lips and into her mouth in one quick motion. Santiago worked what remained of his foreskin back and fed the purple cock-head and glands, spreading masses of white speckles over Jamie's tongue and taste buds. Jamie devoured the wonderful taste of the head-cheese, inhaling the strong scent and moaning his pleasure of the feeding frenzy he was enjoying. Santiago let her feast on his residue for a spell, then worked his massive phallus down Jamie's throat and began to pump his blood engorged dick to full capacity. Jamie was in cocksucker paradise sucking massive amounts of clear liquid that flowed freely from the tip of his massive appendage, ball sheaths bouncing against Jamie's mouth and chin with each insertion. Jamie's throat was expanding and contracting as the huge phallus entered, retracted, and reentered. It wasn't long and Santiago stiffened and with his cock buried down Jamie's esophagus, exploded and the liquid warmth flowed from the pulsating rod. He pulled back just enough that the last few spews covered Jamie's tongue giving him a good taste of the flavorful protein milkshake. Santiago left his cock in Jamie's mouth for a spell, eventually pulling and sliding down the girl's body so he could kiss, lick and nibble on the hardened nipples that rose for his attentive pleasure. Santiago fed his dripping pits to Jamie and watched as he sniffed, licked and cleaned them of their dripping manliness. It wasn't long and he had Jamie's legs pressed up against his chest, his ass spread open and he was feeding on Jamie's rosebud, eating his male pussy and working his tongue and fingers into the opening, getting it throbbing and pulsating as though it had a heartbeat. Jamie was in total lust by the time he rolled a rubber on Santiago's cock and threw his legs back up over the big guy's shoulders and felt the mass penetrate as it filled his womb with pulsating pleasure. The big guy fucked with frenzy as a multitude of Spanish obscenities flowed from his mouth directed at Jamie when he wasn't kissing or nibbling on the girl's neck and ears. Jamie was pounding on Santiago's chest and had his fingernails raking over his back as the big guy brought her to multiple orgasms.

In the meantime Lenny had found his way to the center of the Maze and was ready and reclined on the large built-in queen-size bed in the middle of the gazebo, surrounded with lattice and masses of blooming honeysuckle vines, the lush fragrance filling the air. Pedro arrived nude with his cock in his hand smiling and uttering sweet nothings in his native language to his boss lady. He immediately went for the boobs and large seductive nipples, sending Lenny into total overload. After a few minutes of licking, sucking and devouring the melons and sucking and nipping hard on the large nipples, Lenny shot a load of sperm over them and began to beg in Spanish to get fucked. Pedro wasted no time in entering the hot cavern he had so many times before enjoyed, bringing Lenny to multiple orgasms with his powerful beer-can thick cock. The little guy was a power fucker and had Lenny screaming Pedro, Pedro, oh Pedro repeatedly. The little guy dropped three loads into Lenny before he took his first breather, then was back up sucking on Lenny's nipples as she licked and sucked the long wet black hair under his armpits moaning as he brought her to more orgasms. The male pheromones mixed with the smell of honeysuckle and lingered heavily in the air. Pedro's stiff dick was dribbling and oozing all over her groin as he finally dropped his final load by rubbing his cock against her groin and munching, sucking and nibbling on her breasts and nipples.

Now Michael was caught up in another dead-end clearing reclined and prepared for the arrival of his pursuer when Hidalgo arrived and pulled Michael down on his back so his head was laying over the bottom edge of the lounge. He fed his long dick down into Michael's throat and pumped fast and furiously, quickly dropping his first load straight down Michael's gullet. Without hesitation he immediately flipped the girl over on her stomach, unrolled a rubber over his dick and entered her lubed pussy, pulling her up into the doggy position and fucked her with furry in his eyes and shouted vulgarities to her in his native tongue, once in awhile spewing in English calling her fuckin pussy, whore, bitch and cunt. He was a rough fuck and Michael had to bite and scratch him a few times before he realized that was what the dude wanted her to do; so he continued to play rough back with Hidalgo and call him motherfucker, son-of-a bitch, mean-ass Cuban degenerate, until he finally started liking what Hidalgo was doing with his cock buried in his pussy and began to throw his ass back as hard as he could at him. Once Hidalgo had her flipped with legs up over his powerful shoulders, she raked her fingernails over his hairy back, chest and pinched his nipples until he moaned with additional lust at the rough treatment Michael was returning to his rough and furious butt-fucking. Michael soon realized from what Lenny had told them earlier about liking it rough and tumble that Lenny had obviously taught Hidalgo what he expected to receive when he had sex with the super-rough macho handsome Cuban. He took his job of pleasuring himself seriously, but was careful not to leave any tattle-tale signs of violent sex on his playmate. However, Hidalgo did slap, spank and leave a few light red marks on Michael before he dropped his last and final load all over Michael and then fed it to him by dipping his cock into the spew and spooning it into Michael's mouth as he spit and uttered vulgarities to her. His final humiliation was to force Michael to his knees on the lawn and piss up and down his body and over his groin and hard cock as he made him jack himself off and eat his own cum. For some unforeseeable reason, Michael loved every bit of this time he spent being humiliated and turned into Hidalgo's pussy whipped Cunt Boy. He begged Hidalgo for another fuck before they joined the others at the golf cart. He received his wish, Hidalgo performing like a seasoned gigolo. Michael kissed Hidalgo and gave him a huge hug in front of the others before the three girls departed.

The guys slipped back into their short shorts and immediately went back to work as the girls returned to the pool area gazebo, showered and awaited lunch to be served on the terrace. After lunch they each had a long nap in the shade near the pool and then frolicked in the pool until the guys arrived back from 'The Stables.' All three guys had multiple hickeys on their necks and other private parts of their bodies when they joined the girls in the pool, though nothing was said about them naturally by their playmates. The guys played their big boy games with the girls off and on for the remainder of the afternoon in and around the pool, until it was announced that dinner would be in an hour. Jaraald led the party back upstairs and showed them to their bedrooms where the butler had deposited their suitcases. After they had all showered, shaved and dressed, Jaraald gathered them and they went down to the bar where Roger served them before dinner drinks until the dinner bell rang and the couples entered the formal dining room for their dinner.

They had no sooner finished dinner than Bernard the butler came in carrying a phone that he plugged into a receptacle on the wall and ran the cord over to the table and placed it next to Sarge and said softly, "The call is for you Axel on line two from the base." The room instantly went quiet as Sarge punched the button for line two, lifted the receiver to his ear and said, "Master Sergeant Axel Wood speaking." The others could only catch one side of the conversation, but they soon realized that it was serious business by the responses Sarge was giving to whom ever he was talking to on the other end of the line. The conversation was short, but when Sarge hung up he announced, "That was the Duty Officer calling from the base to inform me that the 39th Infantry Division was being put on 'Full Alert Status,' and all personnel were to return immediately to the base for further instructions."

Sarge, Rolf, Michael and Jamie thanked Jaraald and Lenny for a great time and wished them both the best during their trip to Mexico for Lenny's alteration operation, gathered their belongings and headed back to the base.

CHAPTER SEVEN

When they arrived back at the base Sarge, as a higher ranking NCO, headed to the command center to find out the particulars associated with the call for the 'Full Alert Status.' When Sarge returned from the briefing, the officers only told those assembled that the entire 39th Infantry Division and the 22nd Artillery Division were both on full alert and restricted to the base until further notice. However, Sarge informed the guys under his command that he and five other noncoms from HQ Company were being sent on TDY (Temporary Duty) and immediately assigned to join the 22nd Artillery Division, since the five had previous training and experience in heavy artillery weaponry, but needed to be recertified on the new weaponry along with 22 others from different companies within the 39th Infantry. Both Sarge and Rolf were part of the total group of 27. They were to start their training early Monday morning, so they would be packing and off to their TDY assignment by noon Sunday. He also informed them that MSgt Ross Wright would be their temporary head NCO in his absence pending his return.

It so happened that Tuesday mid-morning, some forty-eight hours later the alert was lifted and everything went back to normal. Prior to

Sarge and Rolf leaving Sunday at noon, both Michael and Jamie were both were crazy out of their minds all boned up needing a serious plowing by their men before they departed. The wild time in the Maze Saturday morning with the Cubans Hidalgo and Santiago was the last time either had any physical attention from a man. They both desperately needed some attention to their lust for their men before their two guys departed for the 22nd Artillery Division Sunday.

At the last minute, before Sarge and Rolf left with the other NCOs at noon, they gave Michael and Jamie specific instructions that they were to keep their noses clean and that he and Rolf had left instructions with Staff-Sergeant Kobe the cook and Spc5 Selvon in the communications department to watch over them in their absence, knowing Michael and Jamie were already horny and begging for some dick, but they didn't have time to deliver a good-by fuck before they left. Sarge knew that the girls would be horny and climbing the walls for some cock in their absence, so he gave Kobe and Selvon the OK to take charge of Michael and Jamie's sexual needs while he and Rolf were absent on TDY. Sarge told the girls that they shouldn't be gone TDY for more than 7 to 10 days, but that they were told to continue taking the valium dosage to calm them like they were currently taking, handing Michael the key to his private room so they could get access to the medications in Rolf and his absence. Sarge told the two horny-toads to hang in the mess hall that evening after dinner and Kobe and Selvon would hook up with them and take care of their greatly increased lustful appetites.

During dinner Sunday night as Jamie and Michael were sitting in the mess hall eating, Kobe and Selvon slid in next to them, wasting no time in directing the conversation toward sexual innuendo and boldly placing their large black paws under the tablecloth, squeezing and rubbing the girl's inner thighs. The girls didn't resist the advancements, ogling at the two black guys, all muscled and looking more handsome than they recalled from previous observances of the two. Michael hadn't realized until now just how sexy and good looking both Kobe and Selvon actually were. The girls succumbed to the under the table advances and sexy small-talk. Michael and Jamie soon were smiling and getting a bit giddy trying to carry on casual conversation while squeezing and stroking the guy's huge bulges tenting under the stretched fabric of their fatigues. There began a major snaking of cock meat down under the stretched fabric until each girl was gently squeezing and stroking what seemed to be massive manhood filling their palms. As the mess hall began to empty, Kobe called the mess hall attendant over to remove the girl's empty trays, utensils and cups so they wouldn't have to walk the full length of the hall sporting the boners they all sported. He then looked into Michael's, then Jamie's eyes and told them to follow him and Selvon up to their room for a bit of creamy after dinner dessert. All four were boned as they slipped out of the mess hall and headed up toward the guy's room.

The moment the four entered the bedroom and the door was securely bolted, Kobe said in an authoritative tone, "OK, STRIP and show us what you got girls, and don't ya be hesitating none or I'll tan your bottoms and learn ya real quick to do as I says!" He removed his shirt revealing his massive muscular development and threw it on a chair, undid his belt and stripped the buttons down the front of his fatigues, lifting his equipment out in one swift motion. Selvon followed Kobe's lead. They both were going commando and their huge black cocks and danglers dropped right out for full viewing. They circled the girls looking them up and down, expecting them to immediately start stripping. Instead, the girls were both awe struck and mesmerized staring at the massive muscles and the huge black endowments the guys sported. Kobe glared at the two pussy-boys when they didn't immediately start stripping as ordered.

Kobe's voice rose almost to a shout and repeated, "I SAID STRIP!" He was pulling his woven military belt from the belt-loops and doubling it over and around his hand forming a long strap as he stood back glaring at the two girls. They wasted not a second as they both started to strip. Selvon pulled his belt mimicking Kobe's actions. Both Kobe and Selvon started swinging the correction devices at the girls, striking them across their ass and thighs before they even had their shirts off or their britches undone.

Kobe shouted, "When I give you an order, you honky cracker-assed bitches, I expectin to have it carried out pronto without hesitation! Didn't Sarge learn you bitches nothing yet! A taste of the belt should get your attention and learnin you two real quick who be yur boss man and own you now for a spell! I hope you two fuck better than you follow orders." Neither guy quit striking out at the girls until they were completely nude sporting red welts across their buns and across their thighs as they quickly moved to disrobe. The guys got some good blows in as the girls were bent over removing their boots and socks, moaning with pain, however sporting boners as though they liked the taste of the belt from their assertive captors. Kobe then opened his locker and fished out two jock-straps and threw them at the girls and said, "Put these on over those boners! There be only two real men in this here room and we don't never want to see those boners again when you are with us. Remember it in the future or we will use the belts on you again until you both learn to keep your dicks covered with only your cracker buns exposed for us to see. It's what I expect of you from now on." The two quickly put on the jocks and tucked their boners in the pouch out of sight.

Kobe said, "That's better," then turned on the radio to a rock and roll station, and pulled Michael into his arms and bent him over inspecting his boy-pussy, transferring the massive amounts of pre-cum coming from his huge black python headed cock slit with his fingers to Michael's pink pucker-hole, working his finger in and around roughly, forcing Michael to stand still and accept this crude and forcefully brutal preparation. Selvon copied the actions with Jamie, only wrapping the woven belt around his neck and holding him in place like a collared bitch as he lubed him up with the dripping pre-cum oozing from his cock-slit. He then turned to Kobe, and asked.

"Kobe, we got any booze left bro?"

"Yea, in the bottom of my locker bro. Get it out and bring it here!" Selvon walked Jamie over to the locker and retrieved the bottle of Jack Daniels and returned it to Kobe. After Kobe took three good chugs from the bottle he put it to Michael's lips and forced him to chug three good mouthfuls, passed it back to Selvon who drank from the open bottle and then poured a like amount down into Jamie. In the meantime, Kobe pulled two reefers and a lighter out of a drawer on his desk, lit one up and passed the other with the lighter to Selvon. The two guys grabbed their captives around their necks in a loose chokehold and put the joints to their lips and forced them to take alternating hits with them until the joints were exhausted and placed in a nearby ashtray. Still sporting their huge black boners they forced the girls to their knees between their legs and fed them their dicks, immediately forcing the 10 inchers down the girl's throats and leaving them there until they were turning blue and pounding on the guys rippled abs with their fists for oxygen. They rough fucked the girl's throats spewing verbal obscenities non-stop as they quickly dumped their first load of jizz down the bitches cum receptacles.

The guys pulled their still powerfully inflated cocks and Kobe clasped his woven belt around Michael's neck as Selvon had done. He firmly told the girls to stand at attention as he grabbed the bottle of Jack Daniels, took additional gulps and forced the girl's heads back holding the loose ends of the long belts up as a noose around their necks, poring booze down them until they were sputtering to keep up with the flow of the powerful liquid. Two more joints were lit and consumed by the four. It was very powerful marijuana and took hold quickly turning Michael and Jamie into star eyed nymphomaniacs, sniffing, licking and running their hands over the muscled ebony guys, turning them quickly into determined and assertive cocks-men manhandling the nude seductive bodies of their two new wards.

The guy's dicks pulsated as they removed their boots, socks and pants and rubbed their sexy black bodies against the soft sensuous skin of the bubble assed cracker's buns. Grabbing the end of the belts, the girls were again forced down on their hands and knees and each led to one of the two single beds and told to hop up and lay on their stomachs. The guys laid over them and rubbed their sweaty pheromones all over their backs, pressing their huge appendages in the warmth between bubbled buns, depositing multitudes of cock-snot, eventually working it with the additional sweat that was dripping from their dark chocolate bodies. The warm room filled with the strong smell of male bodies as in a locker room. The girls were pulled up into the doggie position and the dripping, pulsating cocks were rammed up into their pussies until the guy's huge smooth egg size balls dangling from their long low hangers rested between the girls buns and extended down resting on their inner thighs, registering warmth and feelings of lustful bliss through the girls sensitive inner thighs and up into their brains pleasure receptors.

Michael was the first to start moaning his pleasure, lifting his ass to meet each powerful thrust, until all Kobe had to do was hover and let the hot pussy thrust up and down milking his huge black scepter as meaty dangling balls pounded and sent the dear girl's sensitive cunt into lustful bliss. Jamie was soon making high pitched screams forcing Selvon to yank on his belt noose to keep him quiet and alerting others along the bedroom corridor of their activities.

Well into the session Kobe tightened the hold on the noose around Michael's neck forcing him in and out of oxygen depravation until the poor girl would almost suffocate, then release until she regained her breathing. Again and again Michael was deprived of oxygen as Kobe took total charge of the fuck-fest, hollering tainted obscenities directed to the cracker ward in this helpless but totally lustful state. Michael began to climax and as her pussy pulsated around Kobe's giant monster dick it milked Kobe of a huge climax depositing eight huge sprays of dick juice up into Michael's cum depositary. Without missing a beat, Kobe pushed Michael flat out across the bed and continued pumping her, forcing her in and out of consciousness by pulling her head back up off the bed with the belt and holding it as he continued to deprive her of oxygen for a few moments, nibbling, biting and leaving hickeys and teeth marks all over her neck and shoulders. Michael continued having orgasms as Kobe pounded and raked her prostrate. When Kobe dropped his final load into Michael he rolled off him, spooned up against his backside and they both dropped off into blissful sleep.

Selvon, on the other hand had worked Jamie over on her back with her legs up over his shoulders and was fucking her slowly as he nibbled and sucked on her nipples, ears and neck, forcing his long tongue into her mouth, his huge thick lips locked against hers to keep her from screaming like she was prone to do each time Selvon brought her to another orgasm. Selvon eventually observed that Kobe was delivering a session of oxygen deprivation to Michael and he began to tighten the belted noose around Jamie's neck until she couldn't breath and she was squirming for oxygen and going limp, then letting her gasp for oxygen again and again until he was also in a mode with Jamie accepting her fate and succumbing to the abuse, while still showing all the signs that she was learning to be receptive to this new and kinky treatment from an assertive and rough Top. Jamie's tight pussy milked and sucked three massive loads of nigger jizz from Selvon before he fell limp and pulled from Jamie, having dropped three or four loads into her soaked jock-strap. He pulled from Jamie, straightened out the girl on her side, spooned up against her back and the two immediately dropped off into blissful sleep too.

Three or four times during the night both guys reentered their wards and dropped loads into their receptive cum depositories. About 4:45am, Kobe woke all from their pot enhanced stupors and ordered the girls to go to their own cubicles and get their towels and gear and meet them in the showers where the guys fucked them again under the warm water spray, telling them to make themselves available to them each and every night after the dinner hour. He sent the girls back to their cubicles and he and Selvon returned to their room where Selvon went right back to bed as Kobe dressed and shuffled off to the kitchen by 5:30am to start business as usual - preparations for the morning breakfast for HQ Company.

At work Monday, Mr. Lowe noticed Michael had his fatigue shirt buttoned up tight against his neck shortly after the office opened that morning. He ordered Michael to follow him into the storage room. Mr. Lowe quickly unbuttoned the top two buttons of Michael's fatigue shirt. When he saw the hickeys on his neck, he got a concerned look in his eyes and ordered Michael to take the shirt completely off. When the man saw the massive hickeys, bites and bruising all over Michael's shoulders, upper arms, chest and around his nipples he ordered Michael to drop his pants so he could see what damage had been done to the remainder of his body. Michael hesitated, but eventually was forced to drop his pants and drawers, revealing the massive red welts over his buns and thighs. Mr. Lowe ran his palm over them, then ran his fingers down between his bruised buns and ran his finger over Mike's swollen rosebud. When he did, Michael tried not to wince, but found it impossible as Mr. Lowe stuck a finger up into him and ran it around the swollen tissue, even though Michael had put salve on. Michael let out a notable whimper.

All Mr. Lowe said was, "Did MSgt. Wood do this to you boy?"

Michael immediately responded, "Oh, No Sir, it wasn't MSgt. Wood. I swear it wasn't him Sir!"

"You obviously have been whipped and roughly molested boy. Is this something you enjoy son, or were you raped by someone?"

"I'm not sure Sir! I can't say I didn't enjoy it at the time, but I don't enjoy being all marked up like this very much and I am pretty sore from what was done to me. I hope I'm not in trouble, because I can't squeal on who did this to me Sir, I became so turned on he knew I was enjoying what he was doing and obviously got carried away, as you can see. Please don't make me tell you who it was Sir, because yes, I know now that I liked it and would probably do it again if I ever have the chance Sir!"

"Well, at least you told me the truth about yourself boy. I'm not going to force you to reveal who it was, but you must be more careful in the future, and make sure you tell who ever did this to you that if it happens again where the marks can't be hidden with normal clothing, I will force you to tell me who did it and personally give him a taste of his own medicine. Enough said on that subject. You are one beautiful blond white boy, pick of the litter to us black guys that like pretty blue eyed blonds with creamy soft white skin and bubble butts like you. You obviously are developing a growing taste for kink and pain, but I don't want to ever see your body looking as it does today again, as I intend on keeping a very tight leash on you to keep you safe and healthy and pretty as ever. Now get nude, as I'm going to fuck you boy so you can really feel the pain you obviously think you enjoy when a well endowed man gives you a hard pounding of rough sex. The experience in taking my huge dick when you are already in pain should give you something to think about before you go looking for rough sex for awhile, at least until Sarge returns from TDS."

The big guy was already fondling himself as he spoke these words; his huge dick was tenting his uniform as he pulled Michael close and unbuttoned and removed his shirt displaying his magnificent ebony chest, biceps and six-pack abs. Next he loosened his belt, unbuttoned his tailored pants and dropped them along with his boxers just far enough that his massive ebony 14incher drop out and pulsate with his heartbeat along with a pair of the largest smooth shaved ball sacks he had ever seen. The big man was dripping pre-cum from that massive dick as it continued to grow and the long foreskin retracted exposing the bulbous purple mushroomed head and circle of a lighter shade of shinny purple glands. He smiled as he watched Michael's eyes gawk at his equipment for a minute before he spun him around and bent him over exposing the boy's red, swollen rosebud. He gathered fingers full of cock-snot oozing from his dripping appendage and added it to his already well lubed rosebud, working it in well with his long fingers. Next he lifted the gorgeous blond boy up into his arms with the boy's legs wrapped around his waist and his arms locked around his neck and walked to the nearest section of blank cinderblock wall. He place Michael's back against the wall and let him slowly slip down until his juicy erection was spreading Michael's buns apart and sliding up against the entrance to the boy's honey-pot. Michael let out a low moan of pain as the huge purple head spread and penetrated his already sore and swollen anus. It was a real painful experience getting the massive beer can thick mushroomed head started through the swollen lips, but by pressing his anus like he was taking a dump he soon felt the familiar hot branding iron heat of the initial penetration. Mr. Lowe held him like that until he settled down in his arms and began to let the mass slowly slide up into him. Mr. Lowe was kind and let Michael take his huge cock at his own pace. When the huge cock-head pushed against Michael's little hot button up inside him, he let out a low moan of pleasure and put his head against Mr. Lowe's neck and inhaled his wonderful masculine scent. He put his lips to Mr. Lowe's thick lips and kissed him, letting him know that he was ready. He let out another moan and murmured, barely a whisper.

"Oh fuck me Sir! Make me your little girl! You smell wonderful and feel so good up inside me! I have wanted this for weeks now! You have been driving me crazy for this ever since you started opening your fly and exposing yourself and letting that big black beauty expand and contract drooped over your leather chair like you do every day. I've love it Sir! I look forward to it every day and I can't keep my eyes off you sir. You are so sexy and handsome. I shiver all over when you look at me, smile and your cock gets all hard and dribbles. I've dreamed of this moment many times Sir. Please! Please fuck me and let me call you Daddy. Please Sir!"

"Oh baby girl, I have been in lust for you for so very long too. I had no intention of adding another to my staff until you came in from D Company and asked for a job that day. The minute Sarge and I saw you our mouths were virtually watering. I nodded to Sarge, he smiled back at me, and you had the transfer and job aced. It took a long time for Sarge to get you in his bed, but once you got that first taste of a cock, especially a big black juicer, you were butter in the palm of Sarge's hand. Now it's my turn to share your talents now that Sarge and Rolf have you all trained in the fine art of taking care of a real man's sexual appetite. Your pussy is like a hot soft glove around me and I can feel your heartbeat throbbing against my cock. Oh you are so warm and tight. Yes, call me daddy when we are together like this, squeeze and milk my love juices into you baby girl." He slowly began pumping his massive girth in and out of Mike's anus slowly increasing the speed, feeling Michael's positive response to his quickening movements.

"Oh daddy, fuck me, fuck me harder and faster. Don't hold back; give it to me, please!" With each penetration Michael began to murmur. Yes! Yes! Yes! Oh YES, I love it inside me daddy! Fuck my pussy daddy!" When Michael began to ooze, Mr. Lowe pulled a big handkerchief from his pocked and wrapped it around Michael's dick so it wouldn't stain the front of his own uniform, as Michael ran his fingers through the thick swirls of coarse black hair covering his abdomen, chest and raked his fingernails over the big guy's nipples and inhaled his scent.

Mr. Lowe let out a huge moan and softly said, "Oh yes baby, squeeze and tweak my nipples real hard baby! Fuck Yes! That's it baby girl, tweak Daddy's nipples and I'll fuck your little pink pussy lips until you have a few massive orgasms and really get that hot little ass twitching around daddy's big black cock. Milk daddy's dick as I fuck you baby girl. That's it! Oh yea, my hot little girl has me close!" With that, he let out a loud "FUCK YES," dropped his first load as his dick pulsated and shot eight huge shots of love juice up into Michael's tight pussy. Michael instantly deposited a huge load into the handkerchief, as Mr. Lowe continued pumping with a furry, pressing his huge puffy lips over Michael's, forcing his tongue into the moist warmth to circle and taste his baby's sweetness. They fucked slowly again for ten minutes as Michael was brought to another orgasm, mumbling and moaning with lustful words of endearment until Mr. Lowe climaxed again with Michael working over the big guy's nipples with his fingers and fingernails.

Mr. Lowe lifted Michael off his cock and let his legs lower and find home against the hardwood floor. He turned Michael and the two shuffled over to a low counter. Mr. Lowe place Michael face-down over the end of the counter and reentered him and had to place his hand over Michael's mouth to keep him quietly engaged in their final lustful rush, coming together in a massive flow of juices. Both were sweating profusely in the warm storeroom, so were forced to use a couple of clean white towels from a huge bundle to wash and dry themselves at the large utility double wash-tray in the corner of the storeroom before dressing and separately exiting the storeroom. Of course, Michael spent some time in the bathroom properly cleaning and stuffing tissue between his buns so he wouldn't leave a wet spot in his britches when he returned to his desk. Michael was so sore now he had difficulty sitting properly at his desk. Mr. Lowe kept a dreamy eye on him for awhile until he finally realized the boy was in quite pain trying to sit on the wooden swivel chair and work. He called him up to his desk and told him he was to take the rest of the day off, take a hot shower, rub Sarge's magic liniment on his sore ass and nap for the rest of the workday after lunch in Sarge's room. Michael was more than happy as he thanked Mr. Lowe for being so considerate, as he wasn't sure if he could last for the rest of the workday the way his whole body, especially his ass, throbbed and ached. Michael did indeed take that hot shower and apply a large quantity of ointment to his sore ass before he gently walked to the mess hall and met Jamie for lunch as planned earlier.

After lunch the two went immediately to Sarge's room and Michael told Jamie about what happened with Mr. Lowe the very first thing that morning. They both took another valium and the two spread the soothing salve over each other where they couldn't reach themselves. They each had a couple of open cuts on their back and thighs where they had been whipped and beaten the night before by Kobe and Selvon. Jamie went back to work after the lunch hour and Michael undressed grabbed a tee shirt from Sarge's dirty laundry bag and crawled into his bed and fell asleep with his face and nose buried in the strong aroma of Sarge's armpits for the balance of the afternoon. When Jamie arrived from work shortly after 1500 hour, he awakened Michael and they both reapplied the soothing salve to their swollen pussy lips before they went to the mess hall for dinner.

As they sat eating, Jamie told Michael that MSgt. Ross Wright had been in pursuit of him most of the afternoon at work, even had him cornered and his huge dick pressed against him a couple of times in the back of the storeroom, before others thankfully entered. Jamie told Michael that he was really turned on to him and wanted a taste of that big cock, even if it was attached to a Confederate renegade originally from Atlanta, Georgia. Michael had told Jamie if Ross joined them while eating, he would finish eating, excuse himself as he wanted to shower again and go right to bed he was so sore and tired, and he would be sleeping in Sarge's room where he wouldn't be disturbed if Jamie needed to find him for any reason.

Sure enough, before Michael and Jamie finished eating and left the mess hall, MSgt Ross Wright rose from his table across the room where he was eating with his cronies, brought his dinner tray over and asked Jamie if he could join him and Michael. Jamie smiled and said, "Certainly Sergeant, have a seat." The sergeant slid into the chair next to Jamie and sat his tray down and wasted no time getting the conversation going directed most to Jamie, somewhat ignoring Michael. Michael quickly finished and excused himself, leaving Jamie and Ross together eating and talking. Ross soon had a hand under the tablecloth kneading Jamie's inner thigh with one hand and talking sweet nothings to Jamie in almost a whisper so inquisitive ears couldn't hear his lustful conversation. He placed Jamie's hand over the long tubular bulge running down inside his pants and it began to expand, lengthen and twitch. It wasn't long and the two were headed out and up to Ross's private room. Ross disrobed quickly, insisting that Jamie wait and let him disrobe him, one article of clothing at a time, licking and sucking on his body as he proceeded, until he had Jamie shivering with lust. Ross made no mention of the bruises, lacerations over Jamie's back and thighs. It was obvious Ross had seen and most likely caused the same creative artwork on others and didn't need or choose to discuss them knowing very well that they were the work of a recent Sadistic sex partner. He started out as a kisser and kissed, licked and sucked every conceivable part of Jamie's body, even his toes and the bottom of his feet. Both were drooling pre-cum by the time Ross laid out on his back and told Jamie to do to him what he had done to him. Jamie spent a lot of time kissing, licking and sucking the moisture from the long graying auburn hair that covered Ross's chest and protruded from his hairy armpits. He was one hairy SOB, ugly to a certain degree with huge pot marks on his face and body, obviously from years of picking at his teenage acne. However, his tight muscular body covered in Confederate tattoos and his magnificent gigantic cock and two long slabs of dangling flesh housing his large egg shaped balls more than compensated for his sheer homeliness. Jamie kept returning to Ross's groin area kissing, licking and sniffing the huge treasures until he could hold back no longer and held the foreskin back and sucked the mammoth mushroom into his mouth. He ran his lips and tongue around the glorious glands making Ross shiver and moan with excitement.

Ross pulled a tube of KY from the shelf over his headboard and had Jamie turn around straddling him on his knees. He pulled him back and buried his face between the hot buns. Jamie spread his ass cheeks open with his fingers so Ross could gain full access to the pink rosebud surrounded with a thin layer of bright red hair. Again, Ross made no mention or questioned Jamie why his pucker was so red and swollen or his back and thighs were so black and blue and lacerated with large long welts, a few starting to scab over where the skin had been broken. Ross went immediately to the purpose of the clandestine encounter as he let out a lustful moan and began to kiss, lick and lap at the pink beauty until it was winking and pulsating against his lips and tongue. Ross worked his tongue up into the orifice, spreading the pink pedals into full bloom, eventually adding KY with his fingers and working them around until Jamie was well dilated and begging for the big dick he stared down watching as it pulsated and oozed pre-cum that ran down the shaft and settled into Ross's pubes. Jamie was awe struck as the monster continued to grow to mammoth proportions right before his eyes.

Jamie could finally take it no longer, rose himself and spun around and sat right down over Ross's huge cock-head until it popped in until the mushroomed head was inside and slowly working its way up into tight pussy walls. Jamie quickly had the entire fat shaft worked into him putting just the right amount of pressure on his prostrate gland to send him into overdrive doing the jack-in-the-box movement up and down over Ross's huge endowment. Eventually Jamie slowed and his internal muscles began to squeeze and relax, squeeze and relax, milking the entire shaft and head as it was lodged up against his little hard walnut button, the central core of his lust, giving him the pleasure he always craved from a hugely endowed partner that knew how to rub, squeeze, probe and jab the right spot to turn him into a nymphomaniac in heat. Jamie threw his head back and began a canary bird solo, gradually getting louder and louder until the sergeant had to pull him forward and cover his mouth with his hand to quiet him. Jamie continued his milking action, bringing them both to a massive climax. Jamie caught his own jizz in his palm and immediately licked it clean as Ross pumped this first load up into Jamie's central core warming his honey pot for more juicy deposits.

Ross helped Jamie roll off him and remounted him doggie style, furiously pumping him, only slowing occasionally when he approached another climax, until he could hold back no longer and shoot another huge deposit up into the honey pot, triggering another huge discharge from Jamie covering the small towel they had placed on the bedcovers below him. Ross pulled the covers up over them and said he needed to recharge, as he was pushing 50 and it took a lot of blood to keep his big dick hard. Jamie fed on Ross's dripping pits for awhile before he pulled Jamie into a spoon position and they both were soon cutting Z's. During the night however, Ross did plug Jamie twice more and bring them both off before Jamie dressed and returned to his own cubicle, grabbed his soap and towel and went to the showers for a thorough cleaning.

The next morning during breakfast Jamie told Michael of his experience with Ross and Michael told Jamie he had a great night recuperating alone in Sarge's room where he smoked a couple of Sarge's reefers and jacked himself off twice before he fell asleep sniffing the armpits and crotches of underclothing from Sarge's dirty laundry bag. They both burst into laughter as Jamie admitted that he too loved to do that regularly with hot dudes that left their dirty underwear laying around, especially the armpits of ripe tees. They both discussed Kobe and Selvon, wondering why they had not tried to contact them during the night, confiding in each other that they really liked the rough dominate characteristics of the two big guys, the scent of their sweaty bodies and the taste of the belt they both received until they went a little overboard after getting drunk and stoned. They went off to their respective jobs smiling with the understanding that they would join up again for lunch together in the mess-hall and make plans for the evening ahead.

CHAPTER EIGHT

Mid morning Monday the 'Alert Status' was lifted and everything went back to normal. The troops were no longer restricted to the base. At lunch Michael and Jamie sat together making plans to get off base for the evening. They planned to take a shuttle bus into Tacoma and take in a movie, leaving right after dinner, providing Kobe and Selvon didn't show up wanting their services for the evening. Michael and Jamie were all showered and dressed in civilian clothing as they sat in the mess hall eating dinner early with the intention of catching the early shuttle into Tacoma like planned, when Kobe came out of the kitchen still in his cooks outfit and talked briefly with them. He informed them that he and Selvon had dates with a couple of black ladies they met last Friday night at an all black dance bar in Tacoma, so the two would be on their own for the evening. They told Kobe they were going in to Tacoma on the shuttle to take in a movie and probably would be back around 10:30pm, in case things didn't work out as planned for the two sexy hunks with their new women, letting Kobe know they would be available anytime before dawn with a couple of hot white pussies, all hot for some more fun and games if the guys didn't get any hot action from their new honeys in Tacoma.

As they were preparing to leave for the bus stop they noticed Kobe and a couple of tall black guys they had never seen before just entering the main dining room through the kitchen service entrance doorway. The strangers were dressed in black leather pants, colorful purple and white silky, large wife-beater tees and black boots. When Kobe located them at the far end of the mess hall he pointed them out to the two tall guys. They both towered over Kobe's six foot height by eight to ten inches. Kobe quickly caught their attention and waived for them to come over to where they were standing. The two new Bruthas huddled together talking, smiling, and jousting with excitement as they watched Michael and Jamie's every move as they rose from their table with their empty dinner trays and walked to the dishwasher's pass-through and dropped them off, turned, then walked across the room to join Kobe and the two tall newcomers. Both bruthas were indeed tall, pushing 7 foot, built like they could be All American Basketball Players. The two were handsome and looked deliciously edible to Michael and Jamie sporting shaved heads, big gray eyes, straight white teeth surrounded by huge, sensuous thick puffy lips, large hands, long boney fingers and king size boots. The crowning glory that caught Michael and Jamie's full attention was the huge long crotch snakes and balls, boldly displayed beneath the snug leather covering their left thighs. The glands forming the huge mushroom heads clearly left zilch to ones imagination as to what they were packing. Neither Michael nor Jamie could help but gawk at the equipment as they approached. The two handsome bruthas saw where Michael and Jamie's eyes were transfixed, so boldly gave them a little show by placing the palm of their left hand to their crotches, giving their balls a lift and a scratch or two, then slowly running their fingertips up over their baskets and on up under the bottom hem of their loose wife beater tees, fully exposing their rippled six pack abs and rubbing them seductively with the tips of their fingers, causing their cocks to expand and display even more prominently. Jamie and Michael gasp, unaware that their mouths dropped slightly agape and they both were blushing and breathing irregular by the time they were standing in front of the two and Kobe.

Kobe's elevated voice snapped them back to reality when he said, "Michael and Jamie, these are two bruthas that owns a popular leather bar en entertainment center on da outskirts of Tacoma dat I visit regular. The brutha's names Tyrone en Lamar," pointing to each as he spoke their names. "I was tellin em about you two last Friday night at the bar, so they dropped by tonight to see if what I be saying bout you two is true or if I was stretching da truth." Kobe paused a moment, smiled, then continued, "Hell, come back to my office in the back of the kitchen so as Tyrone en Lamar kin get a good look at you two." As they entered the office, Kobe kicked the door closed and turned the knob to the lock position so they wouldn't be disturbed. Lamar, towered over Michael as he stepped right up and pulled him up to him, spun him around a couple of times looking him over, before he pulled Michael's back up tight against him, leaned down and sniffed his blond hair and began to slowly rub the huge bulge in his trousers back and forth, up and down over and between the cheeks of Michael's bubble butt as he ran his hands up under the loose fitting shirt and tweaked his nipples. Lamar let out a moan as he continued to sniff the blond locks and plant kisses on Michael's ear and neck. It was obvious that Michael liked and was getting turned on as he melted into Lamar, inhaling deeply the strong scent of the Brutha's sweating body in the warm, stagnant air in the small office.

In the meantime Tyrone had Jamie in a lip lock, his fingers worked up under his shirt also pinching Jamie's huge nipples that had been quite visible poking up into the silky material on his shirt before Tyrone worked his hands up under his shirt. He was so much taller than Jamie that he had to lift Jamie off the floor to rub their bulging crotches together. He too was sweating, filling the air with the strong smell of his male pheromones, a smell that Jamie so loved when with bruthas, especially when they were seriously turned on and hot in the mating rut, as a buck with a doe in heat. Jamie let out the low moan of acceptance and clung to Tyrone as he was lowered back down to his feet. Now that introductions and physical contact had been positive, the bruthas put their arms around the waists of Michael and Jamie, turned facing Kobe and gave him a big broad smile and a nod.

Kobe was the first to talk, "Well, ain't they everything I says they is guys! They two of da finest lookin crackers around base, en already trained, likin it rough, en craving us black bruthas wit big dicks. Looks like they take to likin you two nigger bruthas already; must be them big toad stickers you be displayen I be supposin. How about you take em for da night, show em what ya do wit pretty white pussy-boys, and give em a good workout. Just make sure you get em back here before 5:30am still in one piece en without any visible marks on em that will show when they dressed or my ass in hot water wit the top nigger boss."

Tyrone and Lamar looked at each other, smiled, and Tyrone said, "Sweet deal fer sure! Works for us Kobe! I'll call you tomorrow! Just what we been looking for alright – some new pretty white bitch-boys should do the trick, just what we be needen, get things hopping again tonight at "The Leather Hut." Come on you two, times a wasting." He grabbed Michael by the shoulder and Tyrone reached for Jamie, as Kobe unlocked the door and led them all to the rear exit of the kitchen and out into the cooler air of a summer evening in the Pacific Northwest state of Washington. They were led to a huge new 1962 shinny black Lincoln Continental sedan with the notorious suicide doors for entering the back seat. All the windows except the windshield were tinted very dark lending total privacy from curious eyes trying to look inside. Tyrone and Jamie got in the rear. Lamar put Michael into the front and was soon in the driver's seat pushing buttons to lock the doors and make them childproof so they couldn't be opened from any of the inside door handles until unlocked by the driver. The electric window controls were also disabled by the flip of a switch on the driver's master control. Both Lamar and Tyrone immediately pulled some pills from their pockets, spread the girl's mouths open and tossed them over their tongues, quickly grabbing bottles of clear but odd tasting liquid from cup trays and forcing them to swallow the pills. The guys spread their mouths open wide again and ran their fingers around making sure they had both swallowed the pills. The guys each lit up a reefer and passed it back and forth between themselves and their captives. Soon, they were speeding down the highway headed in the direction of Tacoma enjoying the music on the radio and the air-conditioned air circulating inside the luxury sedan.

The girls were each handed the bottles containing the odd tasting liquid and told to drink it all down, as it would relax them. By the time another joint was aglow and passed back and forth between them, both Michael and Jamie were settled back into the cushions with dreamy eyes swaying to the music on the radio, cuddled up next to their guys and rubbing their hands all over the guy's sexy abs, rubbing their nipples and squeezing the long cocks snaked down the guys leather britches.

Lamar's thunderous base voice soon announced, "OK girls, this is gona be a night to remember; time to shed your clothing, sandals and all, right down to those cute little pink pussies. Fold em and put em on the floorboard nice and neat. You won't need em where you be going tonight." Michael and Jamie somewhat awoke from the stupors they seemed to be experiencing. They hesitated, both attempting to comprehend what they had been told, until they were grabbed by the hair, pushed slightly away from their captors and bitch slapped lightly a couple of times to get their full attention. Michael, in a daze asked, "Sorry, what did you say?" Lamar said, "HE SAYS STRIP EVERYTHING OFF - THE SANDALS TOO, FOLD EM AND PUT EM ON THE FLOORBOARD IN A NICE NEAT PILE." When Lamar saw that they both had jockstraps on he added, "Oh good! Leave on da jockstraps. Perfect! They hide those little pink cocks, so if you dribble you won't be making a sticky mess on the leather seats, just in da pouches."

Both Jamie and Michael seemed stoned already, having difficulty removing and folding the clothing and placing it on the floorboards. Was it the pills, the odd tasting liquid, or the marijuana that had them so fucked up and delirious already? Michael was confused, restless and rubbing his jaw where Lamar had struck him. Jamie was already being man handled in the back seat by Tyrone. Tyrone had worked his leather pants open and was dressed commando, without underwear over his hairy crotch. He instantly had his cock and balls flopped out, holding Jamie by the hair with one hand feeding his huge male endowment into Jamie's mouth. It wasn't as simple for Michael though. Lamar flipped the steering wheel up to maximum height, grabbed Michael by the hair and told him to unbutton and get his cock and balls out and start working his tongue and lips over the massive black monster in his leather britches. Lamar was also going commando making it a little easier for Michael to work his huge cock and balls out and free of the clinging damp leather material.

Michael let out a scream and muttered, "Oh my god, I can't get that big thing in my mouth Lamar; it's bigger than anything I've ever had in my mouth before. You must be kidding if you expect me to get my lips around that giant hooded one eyed monster. Tell me you're kidding; please tell me you're kidding!"

Lamar let out a big chuckle and said, "Well ya better try bitch – get what ya can down! Practice girl, practice makes perfect, ya knows! Pull da foreskin back en get to licking en suckin en soon it will find a way to get where it want to be. You best watch da teeth or I be bitch slappin ya silly en loosen some of those pearly whites!" In the back seat, Jamie wasn't complaining, quietly sucking down Tyrone's huge dick

"Now that how ya suck a big brutha's cock bitch. You just needed a little incentive and help, that's all bitch! Ya do ok from now on, or I give you another suckin lesson!" He lifted Michael's head from his lap where he was still busy kissing and fondling his new toy. Lamar smiled, then kissed him on the forehead and gave him a light bitch slap and said, "Ya sure is a pretty one alright – love da blond hair en soft white skin. Yu be a keeper girl!"

After Tyrone and Lamar put their huge endowments back in their leather pants and buttoned up, Michael and Jamie were helped from the car. They were so stoned and doped up they could hardly stand or walk. They were assisted through the back entrance to 'The Leather Hut,' into a corridor leading forward until they reached a stairway off to the right that led up to a second floor landing. They were carried up the stairs into a second floor living quarters. The door was locked with a key so they couldn't possibly escape, sat back down on their feet and bitch-walked down a hallway to a large bathroom. Both captives were wobbly and needing support as they were held over the toilet and told to pull their cocks out of the jock pouch and drain their lizards. This accomplished, they were fed two more different colored pills Tyrone pulled from the medicine cabinet and two more bottles of the vile tasting liquid were opened and used to wash the pills down, as before. They were made to chug down the balance of the liquid in the bottles.

Jamie muttered, "What did you give us. I can hardly move my limbs, I'm dizzy and really fucked up?"

Michael added, "Me too! But I feel wonderful, all warm and sexy!"

Tyrone chuckled as he said, "Just a mild sedative en some magic pills that's gona make ya two real horny-toads fer us tonight. Don't ya worry none, cuss we er here to take care of ya now; just relax en enjoy da attention yo be gettin." They were then stood upright and helped into the bedroom right to the large California King bed and laid side by side on their backs on the black leather like material covering the bed. Both Michael and Jamie were looking up but unable to move now as they watched Tyrone and Lamar shed their boots, wife-beaters and leather pants. They crawled in and lay next to them, rolled them over on their sides and began rubbing their huge black bodies against them until the guys were with full boners and depositing masses of pre-cum between the soft white moons of

Michael and Jamie's bubble buns. The girls were responding with lustful moans and working their buns back against the large black appendages loving the attention the guys were paying to their nipples.

Lamar reached up to the headboard and grabbed a bottle of lubricant, rolled Michael over on his stomach and poured a healthy amount into the crack of his ass, worked some on to his own cock and passed it to Tyrone to do the same to Jamie and his own cock. Lamar and Tyrone worked one, two, three fingers quickly into their boy-bitches' bottoms, then lined up their slippery monsters and quickly plunged the large mushroomed glands and fully inflated heads in, stopping for just a moment after the heads popped in, until Michael and Jamie got their breaths back, then quickly buried the balance of their shafts up into them until the coarse black pubic hair was rubbing against the smooth, soft, white skin of their two new soft white skinned playmates. Soon they were pounding ass with a furry and the girls were responding like wanton whores to the wonderful feelings going on up inside their well stuffed pussies. Jamie, the noted screamer of the two had to be bitch slapped multiple times before he quieted down and just moaned with the pleasures he was receiving from Tyrone's huge uncircumcised endowment.

The girls loved the rough hands of their captors working over their swollen nipples as they continued to be fucked, then they were repositioned with their legs raised up over broad black sweating shoulders and pounded relentlessly, constantly being administered amyl-nitrate so their pussies would go spastically ballistic and involuntarily shudder, tremble, quiver and convulse around the massive ebony anacondas invading and taking total possession of their honey-pots. Wearing cock-rings as they were, Tyrone and Lamar were able to fuck them for well over an hour, as the girls filled their jock pouches many times with massive amounts of love juice, murmuring the names of their captors over and over in lustful bliss. Finally, Tyrone burst his load and sprayed it up into Jamie, soon followed by Lamar letting out a huge groan and dumping his massive hot juicer up into Michael's cum depository. The guys disconnected from their wenches, rolled over on their backs and slowly their breathing came back to normal.

Lamar ordered, "OK bitches, get to work cleaning us up with those tongues." Michael and Jamie loved doing this to big ebony sweaty bodies, first cleaning up the mess left around the cock, balls and pubes, then up over the abs, over the massive Pecs, around each nipple and finally the favorite and most tasty spot of all, the dripping armpits with what seemed like gallons of wonderful fresh wet sweat captured in the longer coarse hair. The Pits were filled with the strong scent of male pheromones that they both so loved and craved often. When the four awoke from their short nap it was going on to 9:30 pm. Tyrone and Lamar went into the bathroom and showered, dressed and returned, helped the girls to their feet and ushered them into the huge shower and told them to clean up good and use the douche attachment and clean themselves up inside as well. Though quite wobbly and dizzy on their feet, the girls were able to comply and soon staggered from the bathroom to find Lamar and Tyrone in the bedroom sniffing lines of coke with short straws.

Tyrone said, "Come over here girls. You want some too I bet! Make ya feel like million dallah babies!" He laid out two more lines of the powder and handed the straws toward Michael and Jamie.

Jamie held up his hand and said, "I've only done that once when I was stationed back east. I think I'll pass, but thank you anyway for the offer!"

Michael refused the straw and said, "I've never tried the stuff. I hear it is very addictive, expensive, and I have no need to try it now. I'll do just fine without."

Tyrone said, "OK! That be fine with me, but you have no idea how fine you feel if ya do just one line. Da nights young yet babes; there be plenty of time to get some more action in before da rooster crows. Ya bitches must feel real good about now too, all ready fer some more nigger dick up those pretty little asses, cuss dat what ya be getting soon! We got big plans for you tonight – you be lovin all ya be getting tonight!"

Jamie said, "Yea, I could use more of your kind of rutting tonight alright. How about you Michael – you want some more too I bet?"

Michael answered, "Of course, it's only a little after 9:55 and that shower and douche really revived me! I'm all primed and my ass tells me it wants some more dick tickling my fancy and getting me off some more."

Lamar piped in with, "Well let's get ya all lubed up again for some more of this fine dick en we see what we can do for ya two horny toad white bitches. Let's change partners this time Tyrone. I think I wants a go with da redhead wit all da freckles des time." They sat on the edge of the bed and pulled their bitches face down over their laps, removed their wet jock-straps and threw the straps across the room into a large hamper of dirty laundry. They worked more lubricant up into their horny swollen pink pussy lips. Unbeknownst to either Michael or Jamie, they kept dipping their fingers into the bowl of white coke powder each time they inserted a wet finger into them, rubbing the powder all over the walls of their intestines and over the sensitive prostrate gland. The girls were soon begging for dick as before, only this time they were feeling gloriously sexy, feminine and really craving cock and in need of a serious heavy anal pounding. They both rose from their captor's laps with boners pressed up against their tummies.

They ushered Michael and Jamie into the kitchen and popped two more pills into their mouths, handed them another bottle each of the vile tasting liquid, then lifted them up to sit on the tiled kitchen counter as they told them to drink the full bottles of liquid again. As Michael and Jamie nursed the vile liquid down, the guys played with their own cocks and sucked and nibbled on the girl's nipples, until both were sporting huge stiff boners, now visible and bouncing up and down when they moved. When the liquid was all drank, the guys put the girl's legs around their waist, their arms around their strong necks and pulled them forward until they each slipped into their waist. They let the girls slowly descend down until each pink rosebud was full of black cock and they were settled firmly into the masses of course black hair. Now mounted, they were carried over to an adjacent bare wall so their backs were further supported and violently fucked as the two guys literally chewed and bit on their shoulders, the smooth white skin around their areolas, and constantly sensitive and growing nipples. This time the guys were not wearing cock rings, but still were able to support and hold the bitches up fucking them like wild beasts for well over 15 minutes. When they couldn't hold back any longer, they each let out a bellowing howl and sprayed another huge load of jizz up into their bitch slaves.

The girls begged for more pungtang, but were quickly lowered, lightly bitch slapped and pinched hard on the ass a few times and told to cool it before they got a good spanking with their leather belts until their asses were crimson red and hot to the touch. They were each fitted with a clean dry jock strap to cover their boners. The girls then watched as

Tyrone pulled something made of shinny metal out of a cabinet. When they saw they were shackles they both tried to bolt for the door, but wobbled and fell to their knees unable to run or walk again. Minutes later they were fitted around their ankles. The shackles had a short length of chain connecting their ankles making it virtually impossible for them to run or walk normally if they could. It was all they could do now with assistance from their captors to shuffle along as the door was unlocked, they were lifted and carried down the stairs and placed back on their feet in the corridor. They were ushered further along the corridor toward the front of the building and guided through a swinging door into the center of 'The Leather Hut.'

The music was blasting and some 50 to 60 guys, mostly bikers filled the bar. Very few were accompanied by women. The place was cooking for a Monday night, most with hot leather clad bodies. The majority were standing at the bar or sitting at tables, all talking, drinking and having a great time. It was a hard liquor bar, but most were sucking beer out of mugs or downing boiler-makers, dropping shot glasses filled with hard liquor down into their full beer mugs and chugging it down quickly, then pounding the empty mug back on the bar and letting out huge burps and bursting into laughter with their buddies. A good 60% of the guys were Black or mixed Black/Hispanic or Black/White. The remainder was mostly White, with a couple of Asians, and a few American Indians and half-breeds. It was a mixture of hardened biker dudes displaying their club emblems, hard muscled bodies, tattoos, many with bulging crotches and longshoremen with bulging muscles, looking like they came directly from the shipyards, the warehouses or their workplace dressed either in tee-shirts and denim or flannel shirts, baggy work britches and hard toed work boots. The ages varied from mid-twenties to mid-fifties, but most were probably in their mid thirties to mid forties. The black guys that did have women with them had mostly white younger blond women hanging on them, not to say there were not some with black girls too. There were a few couples dancing on a raised dance platform near the back of the large room to western music blaring from a colorfully lighted Wurlitzer jute-box. There were four bartenders - two black, one white and one of mixed black/Hispanic, possibly Cuban blood.

As Michael and Jamie were led shuffling into the center of the large room clad in only their jock-straps, shivering with embarrassment, but still displaying definite wood in their pouches to the extent that the head of Michael's larger cock was peeking out over the top of his waistband and oozing pre-cum down over the cotton material of the pouch. Both had their eyes looking down at the floor until Tyrone popped them both hard on the ass with a leather strap and told them to raise their heads and look sexy and straight ahead into the crowd.

Tyrone announced, "These two luscious, cream of the crop white boys are here special tonight as our special guests fur our pleasure en enjoyment. They will be joining our regulars in the 'Pleasure Playroom' next door after we circulate em among you so ya can see what beautiful specimens they truly are. Each has been fully tested by yours truly en Lamar, and is well skilled in delivering both oral and anal pleasures. If you choose to experience the talents they each possess, we only ask that ya not damage da merchandise or leave tattle-tale marks on them that can be visible when they are fully dressed, cuss they both be in the military. Please feel free to fondle their soft white skin en feel their fine silky hair. The pretty blond names Michael, da stunning redhead Jamie. Ain't they eye-candy guys? Be aware that they both especially like the Big Bruthas en you big white guys with big dicks, tattoos and muscles that like to play rough. Both are totally capable of servicing your sexual need. The usual rules apply, of course. Now enjoy 15 minutes of inspecting their sexy bodies. Please realize that da fees for either will be a bit more than our regular pleasure givers across da alley at the 'Pleasure Playhouse,' but I'm sure ya will find it money well spent to spend some quality time with these very special white bitch-boys. Let's hear it for our military guys!"

The guys responded with a loud display of hoots and hollers as they wasted no time circling Michael and Jamie, feeling their soft white skin, sniffing and running their rough fingers through the silky soft fine hair, tweaking their sensuous nipples and running a finger up into their anus making them stand on their tip-e-toes, some even lifting them up with one hand with a finger up inside them massaging their prostrates, making them even more lustful than they were already from the pills and coke that was already working on their nervous system. One of the big black bruthas pulled his huge cock out and rubbed it up and down between Michael's bubble buns, actually entered him and was fucking him flat out until Lamar saw what he was doing and rushed over and grabbed the guy by his balls and pulled him out of Michael. He scolded the big guy before releasing him, but Michael began to follow the big guy around the room wanting more of his cock, grabbing for his equipment until Lamar grabbed him, bitch slapped him and led him away from the big guy. Tyrone had to lift Jamie up off his knees three times, give him a smack on the ass with the leather strap, when he observed him busily sucking cock that was constantly being presented to him to squeeze and fondle.

When the fifteen minute time was up, it took Tyrone, Lamar and two of the big bartenders that jumped to assist to get the guys away from Michael and Jamie so they could be escorted out a side door, through the alleyway to an unmarked door on the adjoining building. The 'Pleasure Playroom' managers immediately came forward and greeted Tyrone and Lamar. Michael and Jamie were introduced to Jemarcus and Deannas, a black couple and resident managers, then lined up with the other whores that were not already with a customer consisting of two young black women in their early 20's, both with large breasts and wide asses, two white teenage blond girls about 18 and 19, two very cute young Hispanic boys, one about 20, the other younger at just 18. They looked to be brothers. There were two young black boys, one at 19 and the other very effeminate and about 21. The final two were young white boys, both very young and very blond. One had just turn 18, the other just a tad older at 19. Jamie and Michael were told that they would be working here for the balance of the night. They were instructed that if a customer came to their cubicle with a yellow ticket they only got a blowjob, a blue tag represented anal sex and bright red was a blowjob and anal sex. They were told after each customer they were to clean up their cubicle, replace the sheet and dirty towels, jump in the shower and douche if they had been fucked, but always shower after every customer, then return to the holding area where they could be viewed by the new customers. It was impressed on them to get the customers off as quickly as possible, as time was money in this business. Once they were picked, they were to escort the customer to their cubicle, take the ticket from him and drop it in the slotted box at the entrance to each cubicle, and then service the customer. The playroom was quite large, broken down into separate small cubicles with walls going up only about eight feet under the high ceilings in this warehouse building. The cubicles ran down both sides off a corridor behind the main viewing room. Each small cubicle containing a single bed fitted with a white sheet, mirrors on two walls and a drape on the doorway lending a bit of privacy for the occupants. Overhead indirect low wattage light filtered down above the corridor of cubicles. There was a shelf holding a couple of clean white towels, lubrication, rubbers and poppers. Pegs hung on one wall for customers to hang their clothing. Tyrone pointed to a red button near the head of the bed and said if they were having difficulty with a customer to push it and they would get immediate help from Jemarcus and another big bouncer that stayed in attendance for such purposes during business hours. Their jocks and shackles were removed and they were both seated with the others to start servicing paying customers that were already lining up waiting to try out the new white boys they had obviously viewed at the bar next door at 'The Leather Hut.'

The customers were lined up for both Michael and Jamie well after the bar closed at 2:00am. The 'Pleasure Playroom' had an unmarked entrance in the alley with only a small blue light bulb above the doorway into the building so most people entering the alleyway would think it was an exit door from a warehouse. There was absolutely nothing to indicate it was the main entry to a brothel. However, just inside the doorway, customers were checked out by a big bouncer before they were allowed through a second door into the brothel. Once inside, the room bustled with activity. The business hours and pricing were posted. It was open from 9:00pm until 4:00am Monday thru Friday morning, Opened again at 2:00pm on Friday afternoons through 7:00am Saturday mornings, then opened again on Saturdays afternoons at 2:00pm until 6:00am on Sunday morning. They opened again Sunday at 1:00pm until Monday at 4:00am.

Once put into service, both Jamie and Michael were kept well doped up and horny, tripping in live Technicolor having each been given a half-tab of Mescaline, a hallucinogenic drug extracted from the button-shaped nodules on the stem of the peyote, and kept from falling asleep and wide awake on amphetamines (uppers) until closing time. Each time they were given pills, they had to drink another full bottle of the vile tasting liquid in the bottles. They each were having the time of their life servicing the rough masculine guy's sexual needs right up until closing time at 4:00am. Some of the big bruthas and white dock workers got really rough with them, leaving them with welts and big black and blue marks on their bodies, before they were able to push the red button and get assistance from Jemarcus and the big bouncer dude that took care of the unruly, mean and drunken customers. Thank goodness the marks on the two were located where they could be well hidden by clothing when all was over for the night. However, they were both so spaced out all they wanted was to be with a man, held and feeding on juicy cock cum or having their bottoms ravished constantly by a big hard cock and sniffing the smell of sweaty males and dripping armpits.

Tyrone and Lamar showed up at 4:00am with Michael and Jamie's clothing, ushered them into their cubicles and ravished them again with their huge Black Pythons. Michael of course was again made to swallow Lamar's whole cock until he was well able to take it all before his bottom was pleasured as the main event. Jamie had no problem taking any size cock, but was also made to suck Lamar's full 14 inches before he too was allowed the pleasure of it up into his honey pot. They were still higher than a kite as they were each then repeatedly fucked by Jemarcus, the big black bouncer and the seedy skinny black guy that manned the main entrance before they were taken to the shower, douched well and showered before they were taken to a separate anti-room and any cuts, abrasions or black and blues were tended to by Deannas and helped to dress. Jemarcus and the big bouncer dude came back into the room and took them back into the main viewing room where all the other prostitutes were seated awaiting their earned compensation for the nights work.

It came as a total surprise to Michael and Jamie that they would get paid for their services. The tickets were all tallied up individually for the total amount each had earned for the night. They were each paid a percentage of that total amount. All were paid cash on the spot, and Michael was handed $250 and Jamie $280 by Jemarcus for their percentage. Michael and Jamie were made to drink another bottle of the vile tasting liquid, then Tyrone and Lamar ushered them to the Continental and drove them back to their barracks on base. They were both handed a few uppers and a few downers and told to take the uppers to keep them awake if they began to fade during that day at work, and that the downers were to be taken at night to help them relax so they could sleep at the end of the workday. Tyrone told both Michael and Jamie if they started hurting with cramps and became sweaty and nervous, they should drink a few gulps from the six bottles they were handed in a large paper bag. They were told the vile liquid was the same as they were given all night long when taking pills or needing liquids to keep from getting dehydrated. He told them it would settle them down and make them feel good again if they got to hurting, and further told them if they really got to hurting before Friday evening to call them and Lamar would drive Deannas over to the base to give them something stronger that would settle them right down, as they should now be well hooked on the strong narcotic contained in the bottles they had been chugging down all night.

He informed them that they now belonged to him and they would need the narcotic from now on to keep from getting the shakes, cramps, sweats and all the symptoms associated with drug addiction. Tyrone made them each drink another full bottle each of the liquid, gave them their phone numbers again to both their bar and their private phone upstairs in their living quarters, and informed them they would be their new additions at the 'Pleasure Playhouse,' and would be working regularly from now on Friday nights, Saturdays and Sunday afternoons now that they were junkies and their pussy-boys and would soon learn they had to do anything he wanted them to do to get more of the addictive narcotic when they ran out. The reality of what they were being told really didn't register as yet, as Michael and Jamie shook their heads in wonderment, still spaced out on drugs and excited of the fact that they were both over $200 dollars richer and still up and feeling like they were flush with money and could service the entire male population in Tacoma if given the opportunity. In fact they thanked both Tyrone and Lamar and begged then to come up into Sarge's room so they could suck on their big juicy cocks again because there was plenty of time before the bell rang for them to get up and ready for Tuesday's breakfast and another day at their Army jobs.

Tyrone and Lamar did help them up to Sarge's room, striped them nude of their clothing again, made them drink another bottle of the narcotic and fucked them roughly for another 30 minutes before they sprayed their jizz up into their new male prostitute's pussies. Tyrone sent Lamar down to the car for four more bottles of the narcotic, as Tyrone stood and watched Jamie and Michael 69ing on Sarge's bed. He got all horny watching them going at it with each other again. He got excited and whipped out his huge salami and pulled Jamie's head to his dick and was power stroking his throat when Lamar returned with the additional bottles of narcotic. Quickly Lamar was stroking himself watching, then released his huge dick from his pants, grabbed Michael's head and started long dicking his throat again until he sent another cum deposit straight down into Michael's stomach. Tyrone stiffened shortly after as Jamie milked another huge juicer out of him right down his talented throat. Tyrone and Lamar wiped their sticky dicks with a towel, buttoned up and left as Michael and Jamie went right back to 69ing each other even before Tyrone and Lamar left. It wasn't long and the bell rang for them to rise and shine to start another Tuesday on base going through the daily routines of Army life.

That day at work, even with the uppers they had taken earlier that morning, they both could hardly stay awake on the job. At lunchtime neither was feeling good as they sat eating together. After they finished lunch and were sitting talking about what a good time they had the night before with Tyrone and Lamar they both began to get cramps and began to sweat and ache all over. They looked at each other and made a mad dash outside to get into the fresh air as quickly as possible, remembering vaguely what Tyrone had told them about the narcotic they had been introduced to in such large quantity throughout the entire night. By the time they both got permission from their bosses to take the afternoon off and met up in Sarge's room they were really cramping, sweating and feeling like they were being punched and beaten. Even their bones and teeth ached. It got so bad they decided to take a few swigs from one of the bottles Tyrone said contained the narcotic that they would be addicted to already to see if it was true. Sure enough, within a few minutes they were both feeling much better. They knew now they were indeed addicted to the narcotic in the liquid as Tyrone had told them Tuesday morning before he and Lamar went back into Tacoma. They knew if they were now addicted to the shit their lives would be dominated and controlled by Tyrone and Lamar and they would be swiftly turned into bigger junkies working as male prostitutes in their Tacoma brothel. They realized they had to either stop cold turkey and suffer through withdrawals straight away or wean themselves off the stuff slowly or they were doomed to lead a life of total servitude to an addiction that would force them both to whore and who knows what else for Tyrone and Lamar for the drug.

They agreed they would lock the vile liquid up in an empty foot locker they found and brought to Sarge's room and chained closed containing all the bottles of narcotic. The foot locker was double padlocked so it took the key from both of them to open. Now they were assured that neither of them could get to the narcotic without the other present, so neither of them could cheat. By the time they ate dinner that evening they were both with cramps, sweating profusely and feeling poorly again. They suffered, but lasted until about 8:00pm before they were into the locker taking little sips on the liquid until they felt a bit better. The little they each took at that time only lasted until about 10:00pm, at which time they unlocked the footlocker again and took a little less of the liquid than they had taken previously. By morning they had it worked out just how much they would need to get them through the day, so they measured out that amount for each of them and put it in two flasks that they each carried with them to work. By sipping small measured amounts during the day they were able to gradually reduce their need. The withdrawal system they devised seemed to be working for them as they slowly reduced their intake, so by Thursday they were down to just a few sips three times a day to get them through without too much pain and agony.

They kept the footlocker chained and locked, but each carried the small flask containing just enough to get them through each day, right up to Friday. By Friday at noon they were only taking four small sips each of the narcotic from their flasks. They rushed through lunch, went to the payphone and called Tyrone collect, person to person, told him they had fun Monday night and Tuesday morning with he and Lamar, but really were not interested in being turned into junkies and forced to work for him on weekends in their house of ill-repute. When they explained that Sarge and Rolf, their boyfriends, would be returning from temporary duty Monday of the following week and it would be impossible for them to work weekends after that anyway, the tone of Tyrone's voice changed and he told them they had to be in misery and hurting real bad if they hadn't been taking the narcotic, and when they ran out they would be begging him for more to stop the cramps, sweats and pain they would start suffering. He told them he and Lamar would be around at 7:00pm to collect their asses to work over the weekend in the 'Pleasure Playhouse' and they better be ready and waiting in the mess hall with Kobe when they arrived. Jamie was the one on the phone talking with Tyrone at the time. He told Tyrone he and Michael were not at all happy that they were given coke and hallucinogenic drugs and the liquid narcotic and what ever else they had been given in the vile tasting bottles or the other pills that made them crazy with lust and unable to walk and function normally, all without their consent or knowledge. After nearly fifteen minutes talking to an insistent and cocky Tyrone, claiming he owned them and they would be begging for more narcotic when they ran out, Jamie lost his cool and finally told Tyrone to fuck off and hung up the phone on him.

Jamie and Michael immediately went to the kitchen, took Kobe into his office and told him the full details of what had happened with them Monday night with Tyrone and Lamar and about the phone conversation they just had with Tyrone. They never mentioned the fact that they had already nearly weaned themselves of the nasty drug habit, guessing Kobe and possibly Selvon had a hand in what had happened to them. After they spilled their guts to him, sure enough, Kobe told them they were fools not to work for Tyrone and Lamar if they could make the kind of money he said they could earn, at least over the weekend before Sarge and Rolf returned from Temporary Duty. Both Michael and Jamie were a bit miffed at Kobe's remark, after what they had explained happened to them Monday night, especially after given the narcotic they were started on. Kobe just shrugged his shoulders like it was no big thing before he turned and started to walk back into the kitchen.

Suddenly Kobe stopped and turned back facing them and added, "Oh, by the way, Tyrone just called me a few minutes ago. He told me to make sure you two cracker assed pussy-boys are around at exactly 7:00pm tonight after supper, right here in the mess hall, cuss he en Lamar really pissed en comin' bye to take you two back to Tacoma for the entire weekend again."

Jamie looked at Michael and they both chuckled, then turned back, dead serious facing Kobe. Jamie looked right into Kobe's eyes and said, "Yea! Sure! It's pretty obvious you got a big stake in getting us hooked up and whoring for those two Mother-Fuckers. You just call Tyrone right back now and tell him to back off and leave us alone or there will be hell to pay, as I already left a letter with two friends with instructions to turn them over to the First Sergeant and Company Commander if we disappear or are messed up over the weekend. The information I put in those letters will cook there asses big time, have the authorities in Tacoma on their asses pronto. We never want to see or hear from Tyrone or Lamar again. You hear! As for you Kobe, when Sarge and Rolf get back Tuesday, he can deal with you himself after we tell him the whole story and the hand you played in getting us hooked up with those mother-fucking dopers. And to think you been passing yourself off as Sarge's friend all this time! We might be no good worthless Cracker Assed White Pussy-Boys to you Kobe, but we certainly are not going to be turned into junkies and two bit male prostitutes now or ever for those two hoods or for your gain either! Now you best get on that phone and tell Tyrone what I just said fucker, because if he and Lamar show up to abduct us again tonight, the shit will hit the fan big time for you three Mother-Fuckers when I don't check in with my friends that hold the letters with the incriminating information off and on during the weekend!" He and Michael turned and started to walk away leaving Kobe standing glaring at them with hateful eyes clutching his fists.

They expected Kobe to make a retaliatory move against them, but he just stood there and watched them walk out of the kitchen headed back to their respective jobs for the rest of the afternoon. Kobe knew his goose was cooked if he didn't make the call to Tyrone before their expected arrival that evening to abduct Michael and Jamie again for the weekend and get them hooked further on possible even heavier drugs than they had already been subjected to so they could be turned into junkies and manipulated into becoming full time members of their profitable prostitute operation.

CHAPTER NINE

Kobe did indeed approach them as they were finishing up their supper in the mess hall Friday evening to tell them that Tyrone and Lamar wouldn't be showing up at 7:00pm, and begged them not to tell Sarge what had happened when he returned Tuesday, as he only had 8 more years to go to be eligible for full retirement with an honorable discharge from the Army. They let Kobe sweat for most of the weekend before they told him at breakfast Sunday morning that if he broke relations with Tyrone and Lamar they might consider his request not to tell Sarge anything of what went on while he and Rolf were on TDY for the week. Kobe told them there was more to the story and he would like to discuss it further with them in his office off the kitchen in privacy. Jamie and Michael were a bit hesitant to enter that territory with Kobe, knowing it would take more than the two of them to control him should he turn violent with them. However, they finally agreed and followed Kobe slowly into the privacy of his office with the door closed, but not locked. Kobe settled into the seat behind his desk and proceeded to tell Jamie and Michael that Tyrone and Lamar had a strong hold on him that would make it next to impossible for him to break relations with them. He told them the two had pictures of him holding young soldiers down while someone else's hands were shoving a hypodermic needle between their toes with a bottle of the drug clearly marked and visible in the photos. In fact, he pulled a whole series of copies of many pictures they had taken showing Kobe involved in the abduction of others he had either introduced to them or taken to them so they could turn them into junkie prostitutes as they were nearing their discharge date from active duty. Kobe had them all organized and locked in a metal box in one of his desk drawers.

Jamie turned the box of pictures toward him and Michael that Kobe had sat up on the desktop and the two started thumbing through all of them. They ran across pictures of Lenny's abduction and some in which both Kobe and Selvon were holding him down as Jemarcus was administering a hypodermic needle to an area between Lenny's toes, proof that both Kobe and Selvon were involved in his abduction. There were eight pictures of other young Army soldiers in the pile of pictures, all young, all white, and all good looking. All the pictures didn't show a needle being put to the soldier, but the pictures certainly wouldn't have been in the box grouped with the others had they not also been subjected to the same treatment as Lenny and the others in pictures with a needle in them with Kobe, Selvon or both in the pictures holding them down while they were getting a fix from Jemarcus or Deannas. There was not a single incriminating picture of Tyrone or Lamar in the box naturally.

Jamie and Michael looked at Kobe with total disgust. Jamie shouted, "So you're the one that got Lenny sneaking out at night during the week peddling his ass on the streets whoring for you're profit, then peddling his ass to make enough money to support his drug habit working the weekends for the 'Pleasure Playroom.' Was it you that broke his arm like Sarge said happened to him during that period of Lenny's life three years ago?

Kobe answered, "No, absolutely not! It was a rough trick he hopped in da car wit at a pick up spot en a rough area of Tacoma he worked during weeknights. Da guy beat Lenny up bad like after he sucked him off in an alleyway; he broke his arm in two places en cracked a couple of his ribs, left him half daid with two black eyes. And the guy was white too that done it." Michael pulled more pictures out of the metal box. They were pictures of Lenny in his fatigues, arm in a cast sporting two black eyes and a split lip. Kobe added, "The kid was a hell of a hustler back then, not a fear one either peddling his ass to the rough trade and bruthas, as long as he got his fix when ever he needed one. When Sarge en Rolf took him to dat Jaraald in Seattle the day Lenny was discharged, Tyrone and Lamar got so pissed off when he didn't show up for work on the weekend, they come after me en Selvon like we had stolen their golden boy from their operation. They whipped Selvon en me good, threw these pictures at us en use em now to keep us setting em up wit pretty white boys like you two is to work for em weekends. We ain't got a chance in hell of breaking their hold on us now. I ain't proud what we do, but we got to survive, as they keep threatening to turn our asses into junkies too en fuckin Selvon's ass until he likin' it, then work him as a whore for em weekends too, since he still young, sexy en good lookin. They say I too old for whoring, but they get me likin' it up my booty too just to teach me a lesson fer lettin' Lenny get away. Hell, I'd die first afor I'd turn my ass up fer any man. You two know I ain't no pussy, en Selvon ain't neither! So what me en Selvon got to do fer ya not to tell Sarge en Rolf what we been doing, especially what we did with Lenny, as he was real special to them?"

They told Kobe they would discuss it together and let him know what he and Selvon were doing was very wrong and serious business and certainly warranted serious punishment. Michael grabbed the metal box off the desk and put it under his arm as he and Jamie turned to start to leave Kobe's office. Kobe jumped up and blocked the doorway until Michael threatened to expose him and Selvon immediately to the First Sergeant and Company Commander. He told Kobe he would keep them locked up for safe keeping, just in case he and Selvon might decide to destroy the evidence. Kobe stepped aside and let them pass, knowing they had the upper hand and he best not upset them more than they already were after just viewing the pictures, especially those of Lenny.

Michael and Jamie realized that they still were not completely over going through the withdrawals yet, so they stayed around the barracks pretty much isolating themselves in Sarge's room continuing to take small sips of the narcotic, just enough that the sweats, cramps and aches were tolerable, always reducing the amount they each consumed. Monday and again on Tuesday, the day they thought Sarge and Rolf might be returning from TDY, they followed the same routine as the previous week, carrying the small flask with them all day, taking small sips periodically, but only when absolutely needed. Neither Sarge nor Rolf returned that day or evening. They realized by then that they best get the footlocker out of

Sarge's room or they would certainly have to explain why it was there in his room, what it contained, and the entire story would come out. They took the footlocker and hid it still chained and locked behind their own lockers in the cubicle they now shared together in the main barracks after locking the metal box of pictures inside where they too would be safe for awhile.

Tuesday evening Sarge and Rolf returned from TDY and were regular horny toads, having been so long away and without any sweet stuff with which to pleasure themselves. They were all over Michael and Jamie most of the night, all four celebrating their return. Michael and Jamie both realized how much love and passion they felt for their two guys, repeating their names as they were brought to multiple orgasms mounted and stuffed with throbbing black cock and juicy hot sperm that warmed their insides.

Wednesday at lunch as Jamie and Michael sat eating they came to the conclusion that they had to tell Sarge about everything now that they both were completely off the narcotic and needed to get rid of the balance of the narcotic, the pictures, and the footlocker. Before they left the mess-hall they stepped into the kitchen and told Kobe that they were going to tell Sarge and Rolf everything that evening in Sarge's room at 7:30pm, so if he and Selvon wanted to be present to defend their actions, this was their opportunity. Michael made arrangements with Sarge to be in his room at 7:30pm, telling him they had something very important to tell him. Jamie did the same with Rolf that afternoon at work.

Michael and Jamie tapped on Sarge's door lightly and entered. It was just 7:00pm. They found Sarge and Rolf relaxed sitting talking, still fully dressed wearing their fatigues. Jamie ran to Rolf and plopped in his lap, wrapped his arms around his neck and kissed him on those big sexy lips. Michael sat the metal box he was carrying on Sarge's desk, along with a single bottle of the narcotic, then walked up to Sarge and dropped to his knees and laid his head in his lap and inhaled his scent for a moment, looked up into Sarge's eyes and started to tell the story of how he and Jamie had been introduced to a couple of Kobe and Selvon's Bruthas and supposed friends on Monday of the previous week. He choked up a bit as he talked, so Jamie continued with the story while still sitting in Rolf's lap.

Between the two, Michael and Jamie managed to tell Sarge and Rolf the entire story of what they had been doing for the past week. As the story was getting wrapped up and Sarge and Rolf were looking through the pictures of Lenny and the others that had been abducted and turned into male prostitutes, there was a knock on the door. Michael looked up into Sarge's eyes and said, "That's probably Kobe and Selvon, as we told them we would be telling you the entire story tonight at 7:30pm, should they want to be present to defend their actions."

Sarge hollered, "Come in Kobe and Selvon! The doors unlocked!" Sure enough it was Kobe and Selvon, both looking worried and concerned. "Well, shut the fucking door and explain to Rolf and me how you two got yourselves involved with these lowlife bruthas Tyrone and Lamar, that you would be obligated to supply them with young white boys from the base to get hooked on drugs so they could be exploited in their house of prostitution. You two stand over here at attention and tell us why you would do such a thing to anyone, especially Michael or Jamie when we left them with you to take care of in our absence thinking you two were our friends, our bruthas, and could be trusted with our boys."

Kobe responded, "Well Sarge, I ain't proud of what we been doing, but after we been going to Tyrone en Lamar's bar, 'The Leather Hut' for awhile en they learn we both from da base, they gets real friendly like en after me en Selvon get pretty plastered one night, they took us across da alley to the Pleasure Playhouse. Till then, we never knowed dat place existed. When we see dem two young white boys in the lineup of whores workin, we both know what we wants. Unbeknown to us, they made an 8mm movie plus take still pictures of us fucking dos two little cuties. Hell, Tyrone threatened to expose us unless we would bring him a young good looking white boy from base to the bar with us so they could turn him into a pussy-boy to work weekends for them. The only white kid we had at da time me and Selvon were fooling around with had only sucked our dicks so far, so he put up quite a fight when we has him spread eagle in da back room with me, Tyrone and Lamar holding him down as Selvon busted his cherry. The kid went ape shit, went into convulsions until Tyrone called out to Deannas and she come in with a syringe en gave him a couple of shots between his toes. Then he calmed right down. When I asked Tyrone what they gave the kid, he says it was just a sedative to calm him down en he be fine now. The four of us fucked him repeatedly for dat entire Friday night. Saturday morning the kid went crazy again en Tyrone called Deannas in to give him another shot as me and Selvon held him still. Lamar took pictures. Tyrone told me and Selvon to go back to da base en leave the kid with dem en come back Sunday night and pick him up to take back to da base.

By da time the weekend was over en we arrived to pick up the kid, he was smiling en hanging on to Lamar like he was his best buddy, constantly running his hands over Lamar's huge basket squeezing en trying to get him excited enough to fuck him again. He ran to us en pulled Selvon into his cubicle en when Selvon finished he pulled me in en I fucked him. I noticed that his body was loaded with black and blue marks, bites, hickeys en his ass lips were red en swollen but still he was a wild and energetic fuck. The kid loved our big dicks en seemed happy being told what to do."

Kobe continued, "Before we left with Lance, dat was the kid's name, dat Sunday evening, Tyrone took me en Selvon aside en gave us each en envelope. When we looks inside we see he give us each $500. I ask, what this fer Tyrone en he say it our reward for bringing Lance to him en from now on we get the same each time we bring them another young white boy to work the weekends fer them. Five smackers each put big smiles on our faces until he told us da whole story. He says that Lance would need constant attention during the week for awhile until he realized he had no control over his future as their new pussy-boy whore. Tyrone handed us a supply of bottles of that same liquid narcotic as sitting over there on your desk Sarge. Then Tyrone says Lance would need big gulps of it during da week to keep from getting the shakes, sweats en cramps, as he was already hooked on the stuff, so we had watch him close like and make sure he had plenty of the stuff when he needed it. He say, if the kid really got to hurting during the week to call the number on a card dat he handed me en he would send Deannas en Lamar out to da base to give the kid a shot of something more powerful to make him feel real good again. He handed me a bottle of uppers and another of downers so the kid could stay awake on the job and sleep at night an. He ended by telling us to have Lance back in Tacoma for work Friday evening." Kobe paused and put his hands over his face and moaned, "I had no idea they turned da kid into a junkie to turn him into a whore for their profit until that moment. I swear if I knowed, I would have never got sucked into dis here situation. The following week was hell for me and Selvon. We had to keep Lance in our room with us at night. He would break out with cramps, sweats en the shakes until we give him more en more of that shit in dat damn bottle. It would make him so horny he kept us both up half the night fuckin his ass.

By the time Friday come, Selvon en me wore out en happy to dump him off wit Tyrone en Lamar. Da next week it get better, as they taught the kid to give himself a shot between his toes wit the harder narcotic that would last for a long time, but he continue showin up at our door at night needing his ass pounded full of dick. They successfully turned Lance into a boy slut, en the day he discharged he be their slut-boy full time."

Selvon added, "Wasn't long en Tyrone start puttin pressure on us, using da pictures en that movie they make to enforce their demands. They wants another white boy from da base en wouldn't take bull shit from us gettin em exactly what they want. We beg em to back off, but those two threaten to turn us into our Company Commander until we deliver dem da second pretty white boy. Dis time they make us stay da entire weekend watching em work da boy over, making us hold him down as Deannas or her husband give him da needle en enough amphetamines to keep him awake en wired. They fucked that poor boy until he was a total submissive, then turned him over to Jemarcus and Deannas to put in the lineup of working whores servicing their wild, rough and lustful, most biker en longshoreman customers. We told Tyrone that this kid would be the last. He grabbed me en said I was just the type of good lookin younger black dude that da longshoremen like to play rough with, pulled a syringe from a drawer en loaded it with the shit he had been giving the kid. He threw me on the floor en with Lamar's assistance, shoved it into my arm en gave me da dosage he had loaded. I couldn't believe that Kobe didn't jump in to help me, but he just stood there in shock, speechless. I was out of my head now, as Tyrone called Kobe over and said he would get the same if he didn't fuck me right now. He refused en was given the same dosage I had. They called those two white boys dat we fucked dat first night en had them fuck us. It was the first time Kobe or I had a dick up our ass. Thank god the kids didn't last long, but when it was over, Tyrone warned us if we ever turned on them again we would both be turned into junkies, and I would be working on line with the other whores, though Kobe was too old to make a good whore, but just being a full time junkie and getting a good fuck with Lamar's huge dick regularly would be his punishment. We never refused Tyrone again after dat night en when the drug wore off we were normal again without a craving for more. Thank god da two white boys had small dicks, but it was certainly humiliating to have em pumping our buns full of their seed. We have since learned that it takes a few shots of a higher dosage to get hooked."

Kobe said, "Damn Selvon, you didn't hafta tell em all about dat shit."

Selvon answered, "Hey Kobe, our lives, reputations en futures are in Sarge's hands. If he turns us in to the First Sergeant and Company Commander, you can kiss that retirement goodbye, and a dishonorable discharge will haunt us for the rest of our lives. Let's just hope Sarge has a kind heart en has a solution to this dilemma we have created for ourselves. What say Sarge?"

Sarge by now was pacing the floor, clutching his fists and looking like he was about to explode. Rolf on the other hand sat quietly nuzzling Jamie across the cheek with his thick lips, his hands up under Jamie's wife-beater playing with his nipples. Suddenly Sarge stopped the pacing and came to a full stop in front of the windows and stared out into the courtyard below for a couple of minutes before speaking. "Here is what we are going to do guys. I was talking with Bernard the head butler at Jaraald's estate this morning. He said Jaraald and Lenny were to fly back into SeaTac and be home by mid afternoon today. Let me call him and see if he has any ideas on how to resolve this without getting any of us involved. Kobe, give me the address of this place Tyrone and Lamar run in Tacoma and I will call him right now while we are all together." Kobe pulled a business card out of his wallet and handed it to Sarge with 'The Leather Hut' embossed on it with the address and two telephone numbers.

Sarge said, "Kobe! Selvon! You two can sit down now, but everyone stay quiet while I talk with my old friend Jaraald." He made the call with his personal phone he had installed in his room. Evidently Bernard answered, as Sarge used his name before telling him who it was and asked if Jaraald was around and able to come to the phone. A couple of minutes later Sarge was in deep conversation with Jaraald. After talking for awhile, naturally inquiring how Lenny was and if the operation was a success, he eventually got around to explaining the situation they were dealing with, the parties concerned and what had transpired the past weeks. Sarge did a lot of yes, I see, and is that right, before he smiled and hung up the phone.

Sarge turned, smiled and said, "The problem will be resolved immediately. It seems like Jaraald bankrolled the entire operation Tyrone and Lamar have going in Tacoma. However, he had no idea that the two were recruiting young white soldiers from the base for their operation. He seemed quite upset and said he would be taking care of the situation immediately and not to worry about any problems with either Tyrone or Lamar in the future. He invited us four up to the estate this coming weekend to celebrate Lenny's transformation from a she-male transvestite to an almost full fledged woman."

Sarge turned to Kobe and Selvon and said, "You two aren't off the hook for what you been doing. I'll give some thought to what punishment you two must suffer for not coming to me immediately with this mess you two got yourselves into, what you did with so many young white boys, especially Lenny, Michael and Jamie. Now you two run along and try to keep your noses clean for a change." He opened the door and kicked them both in the ass as they left headed down the hallway to their own room. He closed the door, turned the deadbolt and turned back to Rolf, Jamie and Michael and said, "Anyone interested in playing with a couple of big nigger dicks tonight?" Michael ran to Sarge and started unbuttoning his fatigue shirt a button at a time, slowly displaying that sexy black chest that glowed with the shine of perspiration and filled Michael's nostrils with that familiar and intoxicating scent of his man after a long day sweating in the summer heat. Sarge ruffled Michael's soft hair as he pulled him up against his expanding crotch snake, buried his nose in the golden locks and rubbed their crotches together until both were panting in full lust for each other.

Michael moaned, "I love you Sarge. I just can't get enough of you! I hope you love me too big guy!"

Sarge whispered, "I love you too Michael, more than you know! How about we get you an appointment with that doctor and get you started growing some boobs for your old man to lick and suck on as he fills you with gallons of jizz?"

Michael whispered back, "That sounds like a wonderful idea. Lenny said they make him tingle all over. I can hardly wait to get started Sarge. Thank you for making me so happy."

Rolf and Jamie both smiled at each other overhearing Sarge and Michael's whisperings. Jamie looked up into Rolf's big dark eyes and whispered, "Oh yes Rolf. I know you want me to have breasts. I've heard you say it enough times. I want to make you happy, as I too love you big guy. I already tingle when you suck on my nipples, but imagine how much more fun it will be for you if you have a couple of big boobs to play with.

Who knows, maybe the nipples will even grow larger than they already are too. Oh Rolf, tell me I'm your girl.

Rolf whispered, "You are indeed my love, you redheaded sexpot. You should already know that babe, but I know you want to hear it, so here goes. I love you Jamie and I want you to become a transsexual for me girl. Will you do that for me sweetheart?

Jamie whispered, "Yes, oh yes Rolf. Anything you want my love! Now give me some sugar!"

CHAPTER 10

Between Wednesday and Thursday Sarge had contacted Jaraald a number of times by phone to see how Lenny was doing since their return to Seattle from his surgery in Mexico. Seems like Lenny had picked up a staff infection in the Mexican hospital and was being treated in a Seattle hospital by their local doctor, but he was steadily improving with the sulfur drugs they were administering; in fact, they had the infection cured and Lenny was to be discharged and able to return home Friday morning. Sarge could tell by Jaraald's voice that he was excited with that news when he asked Sarge if he and Rolf could bring Michael and Jamie by Saturday, as Lenny had been begging him to have the four to come and spend the weekend. In the conversation Sarge asked Jaraald what he should do with the six remaining bottles of the narcotic Tyrone and Lamar had left with the girls. Jaraald told him to bring them with him Saturday and he would make sure they were disposed of properly.

Lenny was up and eagerly awaiting their arrival at the estate in Seattle mid-morning Saturday. Lenny ran to them, throwing her arms around them, one at a time, kissing and hugging them individually right on the lips. Finally she pulled Michael and Jamie into her arms and the three jumped up and down like young schoolgirls locked together in excitement. As they settled down, Jaraald stepped up to Lenny and untied a couple of ties on her silk gown and let it drop to the floor. Lenny' stood smiling totally nude, the large nipples standing erect on her ample breasts and just a long vertical slit where once her small endowment had once resided. She was completely void of pubic hair and naturally a bit swollen yet.

Jaraald spun Lenny around a couple of times and said, "Ain't she the prettiest thing you ever did see, and she's all mine to love and to cherish? The best part is they were able to graft enough skin from her thighs and buns to form a large enough vagina to accommodate my big dick along with turning her sensitive cock glands inside out. She has everything necessary to climax when they are stimulated – a true blue transsexual with all the trimmings so her big nigger daddy can eventually fuck her straight away in her new pussy. Her balls are still intact, her prostrate too, all up inside her and out of sight and functional, so anal sex will still be as exciting as ever for us too. All you see is this pretty little pussy-slit. The doctor says it will be a few months yet before I can penetrate her vagina and put my big dick inside her, but her ass will be open for business in a few weeks, as long as we take it slow and easy for awhile. You know big daddy can hardly wait to start tapping that hot pussy. I just have to settle for those hot lips and hungry throat for now. I'm just happy the operation was a success and Lenny is home from the hospital safe and sound. First thing he did after we arrived home from the hospital was he got me all boned up, stripped me and sucked a couple of massive loads of snake juice down her talented throat. Fuck, can my girl suck this big dick; she swallows the whole thing right down to my pubes."

Jaraald got down on his knees in front of Lenny and gently spread her newly formed pussy open to show them how it spread open with lips of red, but still quite swollen and puffy. He put his lips to it and gave it a little kiss as though it was a newborn loveable kitten, then he rose back to his feet and helped her back up with her silk garment, tying the ties over her shoulders and giving her neck, then her lips a juicy kiss with his big thick, sexy lips as he played with her boobs with his massive fingers and palms.

During lunch Saturday Sarge brought up the subject of getting both Michael and Jamie started on the treatments so they would start developing breasts with huge delectable nipples. Jaraald and Lenny both smiled as Lenny once again confirmed just how wonderfully sexy he began to feel shortly after he started taking the treatments himself.

Jaraald let Lenny talk about it for quite a while before he interrupted him and said, "Hey guys, there is a definite down side to the treatments too. Something you four need to know that has to be seriously considered. Guys, it isn't just the physical changes you will all be dealing with as their bodies begin to change. You will also be dealing with emotional changes that I'm not so sure you will be able to handle, especially while you all are still in a military environment. Michael and Jamie will immediately start with emotional bursts of highs and lows that will keep you Sarge and Rolf busy on a constant basis for months as they adjust to the changes going on with their emotions. There will be days where you two will have to be constantly with them to keep them calm as they cry and weep over just the least little thing that sets them off into emotional overload. There is no way you and Rolf will be able to deal with what I had to go through with Lenny's emotional outbursts that required me to take days off work to be with him as he adjusted to his new female self. Sarge, Rolf...., I strongly suggest you wait until all four of you are out of the service before you take on dealing with there transition to womanhood. Tell them Lenny - tell them the truth now! Tell them about what we went through and what you still go through every so often emotionally - the crying, the highs and the lows, how you have had to learn to deal with the emotional elements, somewhat like a woman goes through during her menstrual cycle."

Lenny wrapped her arm around Jaraald and clung to him as tears formed in her eyes. All she said is, "It's true! Jaraald went through hell dealing with me for many long months as the doctor tried different drugs to control my emotional outbursts. For awhile the only thing that would calm me was Jaraald constantly holding me and making love to me, other times I wanted nothing to do with the sex part. I would just curl up and sleep all day crying. It was a roller coaster ride of highs and lows. Jaraald is right! There is no way you can deal with it while you are in the military. Even yet, I still have times that I get weepy and overly emotional."

Sarge looked at Michael and said, "Babe, as much as I would like to see you with some big juicy melons, there is no way it's going to happen until we are both discharged. Even then, I'll have to give it some serious thought. I'm perfectly happy with you remaining just as you are shooting off your gun like you do every time I fuck your sweet ass."

Rolf pulled Jamie to him and said, "That goes for me too babe. As long as you keep milking my dick with those tight muscles in your boy-pussy, I've got nothing to complain about; besides, you're far to sexy as a boy to be turning you into a woman with handfuls of womanly traits causing me mental anguish."

Jaraald surprised them all when Saturday night he took them for drinks and dinner in the restaurant at the top of Seattle's famous Space Needle, constructed for the 1960 World's Fair the previous year. Sunday Jaraald, Sarge and Rolf took off early for 'The Stables,' leaving Lenny, Jamie and Michael to their own vices. After the guys left the three girls piled into the Beamer and headed for downtown Seattle. They had lunch at a quaint, very popular sidewalk café, then Lenny took them shopping. Using Jaraald's major credit cards, they went shopping in downtown Seattle. Lenny started buying expensive clothing for Michael and Jamie as well as herself before returning to the estate. The guys returned around four and they all relaxed around the pool drinking for awhile before Sarge announced they should start back to the base.

Michael and Jamie no sooner were in Sarge's room than they striped and were modeling their new sexy silk undergarments for the guys. Before they were able to get their new outer clothing on, the guys had their dicks out stroking themselves. Hell, the guys rose to their feet, quickly stripped and were standing spooned up against the girl's buns, their hands on their nipples working them between thumb and fingers, licking, sucking and rubbing their manhood against the smooth silk leaving cock snot trails on the sexy material covering their buns. Needless to say, Sarge and Rolf had all four stripped nude, Michael and Jamie skewered, laid out on their backs across Sarge's bed with their legs resting on the guy's shoulders receiving the full treatment from their men. About 2:00am Rolf and Jamie returned to Rolf's room for the night and Michael spooned his bottom up under the covers against Sarge's crotch until the Monday morning wake up sounded.

Once Jamie and Michael returned to their own cubicle to get dressed for work Monday morning, Jamie asked Michael if he noticed all the scratches, bites and marks of passion all over Rolf and Sarge. They came to the conclusion that Sarge and Rolf obviously had sex with some females with long sharp fingernails during their visit to 'The Stables' with

Jaraald in Seattle. Both Michael and Jamie chuckled knowing that guys will be guys before Michael turned to Jamie and uttered his feelings.

"Jamie, you know as well as I that our guys are going to stray and fool around with women as well as other guys given the opportunity. Hell, just look what you and I did with the gardeners Santiago and Hidalgo at the estate in Seattle, then with Lamar and Tyrone in Tacoma, plus your affair with MSgt Ross Wright and mine with my boss Mr. Lowe. These things are to be expected, as that's the way we guys are when we see someone that we are sexually attracted to, especially now that we have had a taste of the great sex we get from Sarge and Rolf. I suggest we not complain to them about their sexual activities with others, whether male or female, or we will be cutting our own throats and limiting our abilities to do the same. Don't you agree Jamie?"

Jamie answered, "Yes, for sure! I want to get back with MSgt Wright and even Selvon again soon. That Selvon is a real looker and really turns me on big time. Hell, I wouldn't mind even getting together with Lamar and Tyrone regularly if the opportunity ever arises. They are both hunks, truly able to make the bells and whistles go off for me. I have been at this game longer than you Michael. Mark my word, sooner or later both Sarge and Rolf could tire of us, especially as younger good looking white guys come along and are assigned to Headquarters Company. You know, they will be sniffing after any pretty boys the minute they arrive, just like Sarge did with you Michael. They like the chase, the challenge of taking the cherries and turning pretty, young white guys into pussy-boys for black dick. So I say, when the time comes that they start abandoning us for the younger guys, you and I start making our own waves in search of big juicy dicks on masculine men that look to be interested in giving us a good taste of man-sex to keep us happy too. Agreed?"

Michael added, "I'll go along with that! I say we start looking right away during breakfast, as five new non-com's transferred in last week, two were older, just like we like our men and prime candidates for a good romp and some primo lovin', if my Gaydar is accurate. Then I saw the way that new Major Treat looked at me as I processed him in to work in G-3. It was a look of restrained lust in his eyes. I swear the guy had a boner going and I couldn't keep my eyes from looking. I know he wanted me to see it too as he kept cupping it looking at me and smiling as I processed his records. I would jump at the opportunity to jump his bones and warm his blood, though officers are normally not to socialize with the likes of us peons."

As the weeks progressed, indeed both Sarge and Rolf began to spend more and more evenings after work taking off right after supper in Sarge's van and not returning until very late or in the early hours of the morning the next day just in time for breakfast, roll call and work. At first the girls were a bit miffed at the guys, but knew better than to complain. It was happening already. The big guys were either chasing pussy or found some young boys to pursue.

What the girls did was start going to the small PX down the hill and within walking distance from their barracks that served beer. Each night Sarge and Rolf took off and left them alone they walked the short distance down the hill and through a grove of tall pines to suck up a few beers and check the place out for hunks. That particular PX serviced all the companies of the 39th Infantry Division. This tactic opened up a whole new group of eligible hunks for them to scope out – guys from A, B, C, D, E, and Combat Support Companies, not just their own Headquarter Company. The PX was always busy each evening with guys sucking down pitchers or mugs of beer getting shit faced. Friday and Saturday nights the place really hopped with standing room only and guys crammed together getting rude, crude, drunk and aggressively lustful with anyone that showed the slightest hint they might be on the make for some male companionship. Michael and Jamie were not heavy drinkers, so quickly got silly, sexy and very friendly with the Alpha males that quickly gathered around the two. The guys would keep buying them more and more beer to try and loosen the girls up for the kill. The more they drank the looser and friendlier they became with the guys.

It didn't take long and guys had Jamie and Michael's number and were feeling them up and rubbing against them. One particular Friday night the place was so packed. No one noticed as a group of buddies aggressively worked both Jamie and Michael into a corner near the rear exit sign where they wouldn't as likely be observed. One guy quickly had Jamie's back pulled up against him humping his crotch against her buns as he pulled her blouse out of her fatigue pants and worked both hands up under the material and pinched and tweaked her nipples, quickly turning Jamie on as he pressed and rubbed his hard dick up and down over the grove joining her buns. He soon had her lusting and rolling her ass around over the guy's hard endowment. Jamie was then spun around facing him and pushed down on her knees letting the guy rub her face over his basket instructing her to open his fatigues and fish out his cock and balls. Jamie was soon being force feed a big boner and balls as the guy held her head locked firmly between his palms and pounded his dick down her throat until he finally gave one last thrust and unloaded a full hot load of his male jizz directly down into Jamie's stomach.

One of his buddies had his hard dick and balls exposed with Michael's hand held over them stroking the shaft until he too pushed Michael down on her knees feeding her what looked to be about 8 inches of hard dick dripping pre-cum like crazy before it was devoured by Michael's tongue and lips. The guy's friends formed a tight human wall protecting them from view by others not with their party. Jamie was immediately lifted to his feet by the same dude she had just serviced orally, her belt and fatigue pants opened and pulled down with her boxers, completely exposing her from the waist down to just below her knees. He spun her around shoved his already spit covered dick in between her ass cheeks, lined it up with her rosebud and quickly had his entire manhood buried with three quick thrusts from his powerful hips. Jamie winced, but managed to remain relatively silent. The guy held him by the hips and immediately started to thrust in and out like a pile driver until he felt Jamie start to relax and thrust his buns back in response, laying his head back against the big guy's shoulder and moaning loud enough with pleasure that the guy had to put his hand over Jamie's mouth to muffle the sound that would most certainly bring attention to what was going on in the corner.

The group kept both girls isolated as the seven big guys each took their turn either fucking Jamie or getting sucked by Michael. When they were through dropping their loads they helped Michael to her feet, pulled Jamie's boxers and fatigue pants up so she could tuck her shirt back in, button up and refasten her belt. The guys then worked them all back through the crowd to the bar, bought them all another draft, including Jamie and Michael, then left them standing alone together and quickly dispersed working back into the crowd. Not a word was exchanged before their departure.

Michael whispered, "You OK Jamie?"

Jamie threw his arms around Michael's waist and pulled him up close and said softly, "Yea! It was fantastic! What a rush! Let's finish this beer then get our asses back to the barracks so I can clean out and catch some Z's, as I'm pretty drunk and suddenly bushed. You must be too." Michael gave a sigh and nodded yes.

Jamie and Michael finished their beers and were setting the empty mugs down on the bar to leave when two big muscled guys blocked their path. They were the two older black guys they scoped out earlier shortly after they first arrived, admiring their sexy toned and muscular bodies. The guys were dressed in tight white tee-shirts, their fatigue pants and Army boots. They found it odd that they were dressed so sparsely, since it was the dead of winter, extremely cold and almost everyone else was dressed warmly, most in their fatigue uniforms and warm Army jackets.

The especially handsome one said, "Been watching you two beauties entertaining the troops with your antics earlier, then you both disappeared all of a sudden. Glad to see you're both back and looking pretty as ever. We saw you scoping us out earlier, so tell us you're both anxious to get some lovin' tonight to warm you up on this cold winter night. We got a van parked right out in the back lot where it's warm and comfy cozy with nearly wall to wall bed inside. My name be Kareem and my buddy here Jemarcus. We're both with the 39th, Co. B."

Jamie introduced Michael and himself and told them they were with the 39th, Headquarter Company.

Jemarcus suddenly jumped into the conversation, spoke right up and said, "Yea, we knows all about you two being in tight with Sarge and Rolf from our buddies Kobe and Selvon. Out on your own again tonight we see, while your men, Sarge and Rolf are off chasing pussy in some Tacoma bar or pumping those two real young Mexican boys they fancy at Tyrone and Lamar's 'Pleasure Palace' that you both are so familiar with yourselves! Well, not to worry; Jemarcus and Kareem can take care of all your needs tonight. We the best the 39th have to offer." He stepped right up to Michael, looked directly into her big blue eyes, ran one hand through her blond hair and the other circled her waist and landed on her ass, squeezing her buns. He then placed a hand over Michael's hand, lowered it to the fatigue cloth covering his hard cock and ran Michael's hand up and down over the full length a couple of times and said, "Now that should be enough to keep you happy Baby!"

Jamie turned to Michael and gave him the high sign they had worked out that meant troubles a bruin, that these two were probably going to be bad news and could cause them some real problems. Jamie turned back to Kareem and said, "Well we just got our fill of lovin, but thanks. We will maybe take a rain check to play with you two some other time. Michael and I have a very busy Saturday tomorrow, so we need to get our beauty sleep."

Kareem quickly spoke, "Not so fast girls! The night's still early! Here, have another beer with us." He wrapped an arm over Jamie's shoulder and pulled him up to him and Jemarcus still had one arm around Michael's waist fondling his firm buns and the other hand over Michael's hand rubbing it slowly up and down over his huge endowment. Kareem got the bartenders attention and they were soon sucking down another mug of beer. Kareem continued, "We're both all honed up needing some immediate relief for a case of blue balls girls. How about a quickie out back in the van, then we'll get you two home?"

Both Michael and Jamie sucked down the beer, placed the mugs on the bar. Jamie said, "Thanks guys for the draft." He somehow managed to break away from Kareem's hold as Michael did with Jemarcus saying, "Yea, thanks for the draft guys." The two girls immediately squeezed into the crowd. They proceeded to make their way through the crowded floor to the front entryway where they knew it was well lit and safe to exit.

Michael heard Jemarcus say to Kareem as the girls forced a quick release without making a big embarrassing scene. "The pussies are playing hard to get. Come on Kareem, time for action! We both need some of that pussy tonight!"

As the girls pushed through the crowd and finally reached the front entryway, Michael grabbed Jamie and told him what he overheard Jemarcus say to Kareem. They both looked back through the crowd to see if either of them was in pursuit or still standing at the bar. They decided they must have gone out the back door to head them off on foot, or possibly ran to their van to pursue and overtake them on the jaunt in the darkness of the grove of pines back to the barracks. They figured they best stay and have a soft drink and wait for awhile before they took off on foot up the slope in the dark to the barracks where they could be easily accosted in the spooky darkness. They worked back to the bar and ordered coke. As they stood and drank their cokes they decided to take the longer route back to the barracks along the street on a sidewalk that was well lit along the way. Twenty minutes later they started out and reached the barracks safely. As they entered the stairwell to go up to Sarge's room to spend the night together they were grabbed by Jemarcus and Kareem. A ball gag was quickly pushed into their mouths as they each tried to fight off the guys. Handcuffs quickly followed, clicked over their wrists as their hands were pulled behind them and secured.

Jemarcus said, "That should hold you two! It's play time girls!" He swatted Michael across the face and told Kareem to do the same to Michael. He then looked at Michael and said, "That's for trying to ditch us! Naughty! Naughty girls! You two will be punished!" They quickly ushered the two out into the lower hallway toward the back doors. An old army green Ford van was parked out in the side lot. They were quickly loaded into the van and laid out on the bed and the cuffs and ball gags were removed. A rag soaked with a strong smelling liquid was placed over their noses. When they awoke they were both totally nude, lying side by side on a few old army blankets in the center of a room. The room was almost a duplicate of Sarge's, except it had two beds and two wall lockers. It was obvious that Jemarcus and Kareem shared the room, as a weight bench and weights were at the end of the room under the wall of windows and pictures of the two of them in skimpy tight nylon Speedos flexing their muscles in competition, some with them holding a trophy. All were framed, grouped and hanging along the two side walls near the windows above the workout area. Jemarcus and Kareem were already nude with huge semi-hard boners sticking out and down bobbing each time they moved.

Kareem stood looking down at Jamie and looked to have an almost smooth light skin for a black, indicating he was most likely of mixed blood, probably Cuban or a mix of Native American and Black, as his hair was thick but straight, even around his pubic area, all cut short, even his pubes. His chest, arms, shoulders and back were covered in tattoos. They were all graphic in design and really quite impressive. He had most the facial features of your typical black man – thick sensuous lips, big dark brown eyes, but a long thin nose rather than the wide flat see into variety. He was quite a handsome guy with a nice large cock. It looked to be about 9inches semi-hard, uncircumcised and with a wide shaft covered in a darker brown skin than the rest of his muscled body. As it hardened completely, the head was massive, much larger than the shaft. It was a reddish-purple color and even hard as it was, still covered a portion of the glands around his dickhead. It then pulsated and dripped cock-snot like crazy as Jamie watched as it drip, dripped down forming a long string clear to the floor where he was standing. He was smoking a big reefer. He pulled Jamie up on his feet and placed it to Jamie's lips and told him, "Toke Baby! It's great shit! It'll make you purr and enjoy the ride of a lifetime I'm going to give you."

Jemarcus was obviously an Alpha male and the more dominant of the two. He had all reason to act cocky and demand total respect and control, especially seen nude, as he sported what most observers would call a cock from hell. It was as a fire hose and definitely loaded and capable of firing big bullets. Like him, it was a dark chocolate color, and as he stood smoking a big reefer and passing it from his lips to Michael's, it would raise and jerk, then settle down and began to droop and drop down over his long slabs of beef supporting two large hen size eggs, then raise again as he touched and fondled Michael. The foreskin would hang down well over an inch from the end of his cock, and then start retracting again as his dick began to harden and stick out not quite 45 degrees from his balls, slowly exposing the huge purple knob and reddish glands. It was indeed a work of art as it's 14+inches throbbed and spit juicers each time it pulsated with a heartbeat of its' own. He had masses of tight curly hair on his legs, groin, up the middle of his 8 pack abs and across his chest. It protruded from his armpits in a mass of tight long curls. The big guy obviously worked out regularly and had professional help with his muscular development. He wasn't what one could call handsome like his partner Kareem, but he was definitely masculine and attractive except for an exceptionally large flat wide nose. He also had small ears that were not in scale with the rest of his shaved head. He had a long scar that ran down from his left ear to near the corner of his massive lips and another over and through one eyebrow. His big black eyes, large puffy lips and perfect white teeth were his best facial features. He was quite attractive in a very macho masculine way, especially when that head and face was attached to such a perfect 6'8" muscular body and grandiose dick.

He too pulled Michael up onto his feet standing next to Jamie and shoved a pill, obviously an upper, into each of their mouths and told to swallow as water cups were held to their mouths. The guys ran their fingers around in the girl's mouths to make sure they had swallowed the pills. A second joint was lighted by each of the guys and passed back and forth until it was finished. Jemarcus grabbed an almost full bottle of slow gin from his locker, that red great tasting stuff that makes one crazy and lustful when drank in moderation but sick as a dog when one overindulges. It was passed back and forth between the guys as they each took gulps and then put the bottle to the girl's lips and forced them to take long gulps of the tasty red booze. It wasn't long and they were all feeling the effects of the marijuana, and amphetamine pills. When the red fire water kicked in the guys lifted the girls up onto their beds, straddled them and started licking, sucking, and inspecting every inch of their bodies with their thick lips, long tongues and massive rough paws. Eventually they sat over the girl's chests and rubbed their dripping long dongs across the girl's lips, letting them savor the flavor of the abundant pre-cum dribbling from their cockheads. The individual taste and scent of the guy's massive black genitalia worked as a powerful aphrodisiac on the girl's libido. After awhile the guys dismounted, pulled the girls around crosswise across the beds letting their heads lay over the edge and slowly worked their huge dicks down into warm mouths. The girls found this very comfortable and were soon enjoying getting deep-throated.

Talented mouths, tongues and throats quickly brought both the big guys to a massive climax, shooting directly down into their stomachs. They both maintained full hard-on's as they spun the girls around with their legs in the air, had them hold their ass cheeks open as the guys ate pussy and finger fucked them until the girl's each were moaning, in lust. KY was fingered up into them until four fingers were easily being accommodated up inside, massaging the girl's prostrate glands until the guy's pulsating dicks were ready for the next round. Obviously anal sex was next on the menu as they had just made oral sex to so successfully.

The guys lifted the girl's legs up on to their shoulders and worked lubricant between their white buns. Slowly they were fingered, stretching and lubricating the girls until their sphincter muscles were relaxed and dilated enough to accommodate the two huge cocks that were dancing in anticipation for entry into the soft white love canals and begin a slow and sensuous session to let the girls get use to the size of their genitalia.

After a spell Jemarcus remarked, "Well girls, I can see you two are use to big dicks alright, already enjoying being stuffed full of big juicy nigger meat, obviously ready to up the tempo a bit. We now can start having some great fun together enjoying the pleasures you white bitch-boys beg for when big meat has you all turned on and begging to have your sweet asses pounded harder and harder as you scream with delight and your little white joysticks spew cum all over yourselves. You just can't stand to go without a big black nigger dick up you cracker-ass pussies for long. The more you get, the more you all want. That's all right Baby. We will always be here to take care of that constant craving you all eventually have for us big guys climbing your bones. Yes indeed, we always will be here to keep you happy little white bitches."

CHAPTER 11

Michael and Jamie were both wide eyed and bushy tailed by now, really enjoying the lovin' they were getting from Jemarcus and Kareem. Initially they were quite apprehensive, nervous and uncomfortable, wondering if the big guys were going to be abusive with them, since they had tried to ditch and run from them earlier. That not being the case, the guys quickly turned into two big lovable hunks once they had the girls captured and under their total control in the privacy of their room. They took time for foreplay, preparing them for their huge appendages. They started out slow and easy until actions indicated the girls were enjoying the feelings associated with being sexually stimulated while totally filled with their huge black meat. As soon as the guys upped the pace the gals began to exhibit all the signs of the two lustful white pussy-boys they truly had become, sniffing and inhaling the scent of the two awesomely masculine male hunks in rut. The hunks in turn were proudly displaying their muscled bodies and large male genitalia as they all succumbed to their individual sexual desires, feeding on each other like wild animals.

The smell of strong testosterone induced male pheromones soon filled the warm room as the big guys picked up their pace and began to sweat profusely. The strong familiar smell of black meat in rut and sweating profusely acted as a powerful aphrodisiac to Michael and Jamie. The guys were soon pile-driving their long fat hard dicks into the luscious warmth of the girl's juicy honey pots, speeding up, then slowing down, trying to prolong the inevitable fireworks, but they were so turned on to the soft, hungry wombs encapsulating and milking their cocks, they had little control at the speed in which their balls were going to unload. Juicy hot jizz quickly erupted impregnating their baby-maker swimmers up into the soft, warm wombs of Michael and Jamie. The internal molten lava flow brought the submissive bottoms to massive climaxes making subdued squeals of pleasure. The first round of shared pleasures came quickly; however, Jemarcus and Kareem had just begun to satisfy their sexual needs and immediately proceeded to prepare for round two at the delight of both Michael and Jamie.

Jemarcus pulled his huge shaft from between Michael's hot buns, lifted her up onto his bed face down, worked a pillow up under her mid section and quickly mounted her again. He immediately began doing powerful push-ups until sweat began dripping off him and raining down onto Michael's back and buns. Finally, dripping wet with perspiration, he dropped to his knees and forearms over Michael and rubbed his sweaty body back and forth over the soft white skin, his face, lips and nose buried in the soft, sweet smelling blond hair covering Michael's head. He continued fucking her sweet ass until his muscles were bulging and he stiffened, throwing his head back and letting out a loud 'Fuck YES,' dropping another massive load of baby makers into Michael's already hot and juicy womb. This caused Michael to climax sending hot sperm down on to the towel they had spread over the bedclothes. Jemarcus rolled over on to his side still joined with his playmate, taking her with him. He continued nuzzling his nose into her neck and golden locks, inhaling her fresh scent deeply, letting out a loud masculine moan before stating the obvious.

"You be one hot bitch girl! I can tell you love the feel of my dick fuckin your sweet cracker ass!"

"Mmmm Yes - I sure do love your big black juicer. It's bigger around than any I have experienced for some time, and really felt so good constantly spreading and rubbing on my hot button. I loved the way it gets me off and want a lot more. Your strong masculine scent is a natural aphrodisiac to me too. You smell so great all I want to do is sniff, lick, suck and taste of you all over Jemarcus! You're definitely the ALPHA-MAN!"

"Well, well – that can be arranged - coming right up baby-cakes!" He pulled his still semi-hard cock from Michael and rolled over on his back, lifted and turned Michael so he was laying face down on top of his dripping wet tuffs of wiry black hair and skin on his muscled pecks, abs and stomach. He put one arm up over his head as his other guided Michael's head and face into the coarse hair in his armpit and whispered, "This is all for you babe. Enjoy baby after you give me some sugar!" Michael inhaled J's pit, rubbed his face in the dripping wet mass of hair and then turned her head just enough to join her lips with J's huge, puffy black lips, the kind she so loved tasting on black guys. Jemarcus nibbled on Michael's lower lip after she tasted his tongue and the sweet tasting saliva inside his mouth. He then placed her face back in his pit. He just let Michael have her way licking and sniffing the sweat that saturated his body. Special attention was paid to the big guy's dripping, hairy armpits and his huge king size erect nips. Michael was intoxicated tongue lapping her way down over J's chest, abs, naval and into the dense black hair surrounding the massive cock and balls. She devoured every bit of salty moisture she could find, finally traveling down a thigh, calve and foot. She licked and sucked J's long toes admiring how each was perfectly formed into separate joints as were those on fingers. She then switched to J's other foot and worked her way back up to the prize. She began by holding the long thick blind meat shaft up with one hand and licking it from base to the long skin covering the massive head. The final delight was working her tongue down into the inch long loose tube of excess skin and working her tongue around and around until the skin started to pull back as the shaft expanded and began to pulsate from the pleasurable stimulation. Slowly the foreskin retracted, exposing the huge mushroom head and reddish purple glands, allowing Michael to slurp and lick, taste and smell to her heart's content all the juices of their mixed body fluids. Michael devoured all traces of the heady mixture. She showed all the signs of a dedicated Cock Connoisseur.

Jemarcus moaned, "Suck it baby! Oh! Make daddy proud of his pretty blond cocksucker." The huge veins running down and around the full length of J's black cock-shaft were pulsating at a speed matching his heartbeat. "Yea baby - swallow it now! Oh yes, just like that! Oh FUCK is that good baby! It won't be long and daddy will deliver a big creamy protein shake for you baby! OH YEA – hear it comes! OH FUCK YES!" The big guy's entire body began to involuntarily tremble and jolt as Michael's throat and mouth filled with massive blasts of delicious creamy protein fit for a queen.

Michael was devouring the juicy dessert, moaning, face totally mounted over the 'Great Black Deliverer,' until it became too painfully sensitive for Jemarcus to endure. He grabbed Michael by the ears, lifted her mouth off his cock and directed her head back up to settle into his moist armpit.

"Inhale baby, inhale my strong scent. Rest there while I recharge! Then big daddy will let you ride the pony for awhile and get you all emotional again. Inhale me good baby, soon you will crave big daddy's scent and taste and want his big dick inside that tight, hot boy-pussy and really get addicted to me putting the meat to you and filling you with my jizz. Wouldn't you like that Michael baby?"

"Um huh, I sure could fall for you big time Daddy Jemarcus – you are very special to me already, but Sarge is my number one guy and I'm committed to his happiness as long as he wants me and treats me fairly.

"Well, you must know by now he and Raul are cheating on you two girls pretty regularly, so I figure maybe I have a chance to steal your heart away from Sarge and put you in my arms regularly, maybe even full time. We will see! I may have to challenge him for you very soon and may the best man win you babe. That would be me of course, hands down – no contest! You let me know when you've had enough of his infidelity and I'll make my move. In the meantime, I will be here for you when ever you need big daddy tickling your fancy making you feel special!"

Kareem all this time has Jamie laid out on her back on the leather covered weight bench, holding her legs up and spread out wide being held by his long arms as he butt fucks her white ass. Jamie's eyes are closed, her mouth gaped open drooling, looking as though she is enjoying Kareem's mastery of the art of corn holing and keeping a girl on the edge of orgasm and in the need for all the pleasure she can get from a sexy good looking black stud like him. She is in total bliss and oblivious to everything other than the sexual pleasure she is feeling running through her entire body.

Jamie is softly muttering, "Fuck me harder Kareem. Oh yea, that's it. You got it now stud. Oh Yes, just please don't stop! Oh fuck, I'm gona cum." Jamie suddenly shoots a long shot of creamy jizz, which goes over her head and is soon running down the adjoining wall, followed by four more gushers that cover her own face, neck and chest. She is trembling and her pussy muscles are pulsating with each ejaculation.

Jamie's internal muscle action instantly takes Kareem over the top. How could he not shoot his load with the constant milking muscles working their magic along his dick – there was no holding back. He stiffens and drops his powerful load of wiggly swimmers up into Jamie's womb. As they slowly return to Earth from the Milky Way, Kareem lowers Jamie's legs to the floor and helps her to her feet. She suddenly is on wobbly feet and leans on Kareem for support. He pops Jamie lovingly on the ass cheeks and leads her to his bed where they cuddle together hugging and kissing and are soon joined again on their sides enjoying a slow session of blissful lovemaking.

During the night between short naps, the guys take the girls through many more passionate orgasms. The Saturday morning sun is rising in the eastern sky as Jemarcus nudges Michael awake and says, "Rise and shine babe; daddy needs some food, so get your buns up and we will shower, then get some grub in the mess hall." When he looked over to roust Kareem and Jamie to join them they were already up and awake, obviously already down the hall in the showers, since their cloths still lay draped over the desk chair. Jemarcus and Michael rushed to the showers and it wasn't long and the four were in the mess hall leisurely consuming enough calories to replenish all the energy they had burned during the night.

After breakfast, Jamie and Michael told the guys they needed to walk across the centralized parade ground back to HQ's Company so they could clean up a bit more, change clothing and check on a few things that needed taken care, like laundry and cleaning up their cubicle, etc. They didn't get any flack from either Jemarcus or Kareem after they agreed to let them walk them over to their barracks so they could see where the girl's cubicle was located. Before the guys left the girls to their chores and wandered back to their own barracks at Co B, they asked them if they wanted to play some more that evening, to show up at their room at 5:00pm and the four could eat dinner together in their mess hall again and plan another evening together playing pony games. A big hug, a kiss and a swift pop on their asses from the two big guys and they were off headed back across the large parade ground that tied the individual company barracks of the 39th Infantry together.

Michael and Jamie immediately checked to see if Sarge and Rolf were back in their rooms from their evening escapades. They found no trace of the guys or any indication that they had returned and spent the night in their barracks rooms, so they spent the remainder of Saturday morning cleaning and trudging their dirty laundry down the road a couple of blocks to the Laundromat, finishing up and returning to the barracks just before lunchtime. They showered and cleaned themselves up real well, slipped into some of the sexy silk underclothing and new expensive civvies that Lenny had purchased for them in Seattle and went down to the mess hall for lunch to see what affect they would have on the men present. They were really quite impressed with how many guys turned their heads and stared at them as they went through the chow line with their trays and sauntered down the isles finding a vacant table in their new tight fitting outfits that showed off their finest physical attributes. While they were eating they discussed their options for the evening and the weekend should Sarge and Rolf not show up soon to be with them. They both realized that unless Sarge and Rolf returned before 5:00, Jemarcus and Kareem would most likely be their companions again tonight, which they both agreed would be just fine. They also thought they might get the telephone number from Kobe for Tyrone and Lamar at the 'Leather Hut' and 'Pleasure Playhouse' in Tacoma, call them and see if they wanted to come by and pick them up to play over the weekend. Before they left the mess hall they did get Kobe to give them the telephone number for Tyrone and Lamar. They called from Kobe's office phone to Tacoma to talk with Tyrone and Lamar, but an answering machine took the call. They left a message stating they would be interested in spending the weekend with them should they be interested, so they would be calling them back around 4:00pm to talk.

When they left Kobe's office and the mess hall they still had no idea what they would be doing that evening, or the weekend, as a matter of fact, but still hopeful that their guys, Sarge and Rolf would be back from wherever they were soon and reunite with them for the weekend. They headed down the corridor toward the stairwell leading to the second floor and their cubicle to take a leisurely nap in preparation for the Saturday night ahead, as they didn't get much rest the night before in the company of Jemarcus and Kareem. They both stripped, hung up their expensive clothing so they wouldn't get wrinkled and crawled into their cots for a leisurely after lunch nap.

They were rudely awakened at about 4:00pm by the sound of the all alert signal coming through the PA system, followed by the First Sergeant's voice announcing that the 39th Infantry Division was being placed on full alert and all personnel were restricted to base and those off base were to be notified and return to headquarters in uniform for further instructions immediately.

Needless to say, by the end of the following week when talks between President Kennedy and Soviet leader Khrushchev reached the boiling stage, the cold war escalated into what became know as the Berlin Crisis. That 1961 event deployed the entire 39th Infantry Division in a massive airlift operation to Germany. The 39th was packed up, airlifted via South Carolina, then to the Azores, and finally landing in Frankfort, Germany and trucked to Wildflicken, near Fulda, just a short distance from the border separating East and West Germany. Michael and Jamie were devastated when Sarge and Rolf were reassigned and again placed on Temporary Duty (TDY) with the 22nd Artillery Division and deployed to West Berlin. Michael and Jamie quickly realized that they wouldn't be seeing Sarge or Rolf for some time, possibly never if we went to war.

By the fourth evening in Wildflicken, Michael and Jamie both craved the attention of a man, so shortly after chow that evening they trudged through the snow in the dead of winter and found their way to a local beer pub, walking distance of their barracks. They stopped at the very first one they encountered in the small village. Once inside the customers consisted of some male locals and a few West German soldiers that were most likely stationed nearby along the East/West German border, none of which spoke more than a few words of English. At first the German guys ignored them, but as soon as the strong dark German beer, quite high in alcohol kicked in, it wasn't long and Michael and Jamie were showing their true colors and coming on to all the hunky guys, especially the German soldiers in uniform. The language barrier no longer seemed to be a problem with communicating with the Germans for Michael and Jamie, now soused up and turned into a couple of sexy effeminate exhibitionists. They quickly became quite welcome and popular with all the Germans, the older owner of the pub and his two bartenders, but especially with the macho soldiers. The two were bought more and more dark beer by the Germans until they were shit-faced drunk, loose, and letting the guys know exactly what they wanted. They danced with guys, letting them squeeze and fondle them as they rubbed their raging hard-on's against the two obvious American gay-boys. Acting like two girls in heat and enjoying the physical stimulation they were receiving from the Germans, the girls began to do a slow strip to the music.

Once Michael and Jamie were down to their tight-e-white-e undergarments, and a couple of the Alpha male soldiers had their big dicks out and preparing to rut the two right their in the center of the pub, the older tavern owner and the largest of the two bartenders stepped in and grabbed Michael and Jamie by the nap of their necks and the waistband on their shorts, pulling them away from the two Alpha male soldiers. The old tavern owner made an announcement in their native language that neither Michael or Jamie understood, but the others were soon whistling and shouting with excitement. He and the one bartender then ushered the two down a hallway and into a large storeroom in the back of the pub, locked the door behind them and stripped the girls of their boxers rendering the two completely nude. They were led to the back and pushed toward a couple of mattresses spread on the floor covered with clean sheets. The bartender began to talk in broken English telling them they would be the entertainment and pussy-boy whores for the night, since they were so eager, earning half of what would be collected from the guys for their special services. He pointed to a shelf containing towels, lube and rubbers. Off to one side was a toilet, wash basin and stall shower with soap. He smiled at the two, popped them each on the ass a couple of times and he and the old tavern owner grabbed their boxers, put them to their noses, sniffed the undergarments and the old guy grabbed both and put them in his back pocket. They left leaving Michael and Jamie standing looking at each other in total surprise. They heard the door lock as they exited. Jamie and Michael smiled at each other, then immediately began to prepare themselves for an evening of physical delights. It wasn't long and the door opened and the two Alpha male soldiers entered that took the lead while they were on the dance floor stripping. The two big guys pulled their dripping cocks out walked toward the girls, waiving their huge endowments at the two until they were pushed up against them pushing the two down on their knees with their faces buried in the guy's crotches. It didn't take long and the two German soldiers dropped their creamy jizz with the sound of a massive groan of pleasure.

The old tavern owner in the meantime had entered the room and was sitting in a chair monitoring the proceedings making sure only the services purchased were what was delivered to each customer as he sniffed and chewed on the girl's boxers he pulled from his rear pocket. He shouted in German to the two Alpha male soldiers after they fed their jizz to the girls. They backed off, put their dicks back in their pants and left the room glaring at the tavern owner as they exited. Two more guys entered as they were leaving, and the girls again blew the two at the command of the old man running the show. It seemed like that was all they would be doing until everyone took their first turn. The two Alpha Male soldiers first at the girls were soon back paying the old guy for a second round with the girls. This time they stripped nude and started licking and sucking on the girl's asses and rosebuds, pinching their nipples and getting them all lustful and begging to get fucked. That's all it took for the guys to throw the two bitches on their backs, lift there legs up over their shoulders and mount them quickly. They fucked for a good twenty minutes before the old guy shouted something to them and they picked up speed and soon dropped a huge load of baby makers up into Michael and Jamie's hot money-maker sexy bottoms. The guys dressed and the next pair that entered also stripped and fucked their hot asses as well. Each of the following pair, some receiving blow jobs, some only screwing the two, but some received both services with Michael and Jamie before the old guy would shout and the guys would dress and exit. This went on until 2:00am – closing time. The old man was so worked up at that time himself, he stepped up to Jamie and pulled out his dick as Jamie dropped to her knees and quickly brought the old guy's dick to a swift climax. The old man pulled their shorts out of his pocket, sniffed them again and handed them to the two, just as the two bartenders entered the room with their other clothing. They both stripped and took their pleasures with Michael and Jamie before dressing and returning to their closing duties up front.

Just as Michael and Jamie were finished showering and dressing the old man grabbed them both by the arms and led them back to the now empty pub, except for the three of them and the two bartenders. The bartender that spoke English handed both Michael and Jamie a wad of German marks which they were told amounted to $60 each. The bartender then acted as interpreter for the old tavern owner stating that he would like to have them come back every evening they could, especially the weekends and work the back room. He said the word would get around and on weekends they might easily earn $150 to $200 each per night. They were more interested in the sex than the money, but didn't refuse the old man's monetary offer to guarantee their return each evening. They threw their arms around the old man, kissed him and were soon back at their barracks tucked into their own bunks dreaming of things to come.

Michael and Jamie physically bonded with the West German Soldiers and were treated to some wild sex during the following weeks. The big masculine German hunks naturally always were the fuckers, Michael and Jamie the receptive, delighted and lustfully excited fuckees. They learned in that storeroom that nearly every one of the German soldiers they serviced sported the natural long lace curtains (not circumcised), were well hung and really knew how to fuck ass and put a smile on a girl's face. For nearly eight weeks while they were stationed in Wildflicken they gravitated back to that beer joint each night getting shit faced on the strong beer and graciously servicing the horny West German troops that seemed to gather there in larger and larger numbers once the word got around about the special talents of the two beautiful young US Army soldiers.

Michael and Jamie did get away on a couple of weekends to travel a bit. One weekend in particular while they were checking out the gay bars in Frankford, they were aggressively pursued by a good looking German man, probably in his early thirties, in a bar called 'The Red Fox.' After Michael and Jamie became a bit tipsy and loosened up on the strong dark beer, the man easily talked them into accompanying him to his nearby apartment on foot. All went well until he ushered them through the bedroom, the only way into the bathroom in the small second story apartment. The guy didn't speak a word of English. As they were led through the darkened bedroom laughing in route to the bathroom, the guy tripped on something and fell out flat on the bed. A woman, obviously his girl or his wife, instantly awoke, rubbed her eyes and looked up at the three. He said a few words to her in German, kissed her and climbed off the bed. She looked up at Michael and Jamie, said something with another big smile, then turned over and went right back to sleep. Once he got Michael and Jamie into the bathroom he stood over the toilet, pulled out his cock, worked the long foreskin back off the head and began to pee, letting out a few moans as it drained. He left his huge flaccid cock hanging loose, then slowly started jacking it to its' full blown glory. He then slowly turned and stepped aside motioning for both Michael and Jamie to do the same. The minute Michael had finished, he grabbed him into his arms, spun him around, loosened Michael's belt and lowered his pants and boxers down to just above the knees in what seemed like an instant. He rubbed his hardened cock up and down between Michael's bare buns spreading the steady stream of cock-snot with one hand where needed as the other hand ran up under his shirt and tweaked his nipples until Michael was turned on to his manipulations and softly moaning with his head thrown back on the guy's shoulder. The guy pulled his foreskin back all the way off the glands on the mushroomed head and rubbed the steady supply of pre-cum with his fingers over the head of his dick and into Michael's pulsating rosebud. He pushed Michael face down over the countertop of the lavatory and lined his dick up with the target. In one huge thrust of his pelvis, he roughly mounted Michael and began to hump his ass spouting what had to be obscenities in German, stressing certain words as he took total control of Michael. He lowered his head down on the back of Michael's neck, held him in place with his teeth dug into his shoulder as a dog would do with his bitch, until Michael adjusted to the rough treatment he was receiving. The big guy didn't last long before he stiffened and dropped his huge load of jizz with a loud grunt. He pulled quickly, still sexually aroused and fully boned. He immediately pulled down Jamie's pants and shorts. He spat in his palm and rubbed it over his dick, hacked again on his finger and worked three up into Jamie before he pushed him up against the wall and mounted him just as roughly as he had with Michael and again spouting non-stop German obscenities, only louder, as though he was working off his hostilities as he fucked a queer boy. It took much longer this time for him to drop his juicer into Jamie. After he climaxed, he pulled a handful of toilet tissue off the roll, wiped his dick clean, pulled off more and stuffed it in the crack of each of their asses to catch any wet cum seepage discharges, had them pull up their shorts and pants and quickly led them back through the bedroom to the stairway leading to the front door. He literally pushed them out spouting something in German as he shut the door leaving them on the stoop in the cold on this winter night. The two looked at each other and started laughing. They discussed what had just happened, then walked back to 'The Red Fox' and had a few more dark beers before they went on their way back to a cheap hotel room they had rented earlier that day for the night. The two kissed and made out, finally 69ing and blowing each other before they curled up together and dropped off to sleep until mid-morning.

Once things settled down along the borders of East/West Berlin and East/West Germany and the East Germans started building the Berlin

Wall to keep the East Berlin population from crossing the boarder into West Berlin and West Germany on a daily basis for higher paying jobs and a better life, the crisis was over and the 39th returned to Fort Lewis, Washington. Sarge and Rolf soon were back off TDY with the 22nd Artillery and very glad to be back and humping Michael and Jamie. What ever happened to Sarge and Rolf while they were with the 22nd Artillery changed them considerably. The two seemed perfectly content and happy taking their pleasures with Michael and Jamie every night of the week, as well as on the weekends when the four would pack into the old van and run up to Seattle to spend quality time together with Jaraald and Lenny.

Three months later, the end of August 1962, Michael's 18 month term of active duty with the US Army expired and he was honorably discharged. It was pre-arranged by Sarge and Jaraald that he would spend the next six months in the big house in Seattle and start going through the medical treatments to become a transsexual, awaiting Sarge's honorable discharge. Sarge spent every moment possible before his discharge with Michael in the big house in Seattle comforting and making love to him. Lenny was a big help, acting like his big sister, helping him through the mood swings and discomforts that he himself had experienced. Between Lenny and Jaraald, Michael was kept happy and comforted when Sarge was on base completing his active duty. They had become such a well knit family that Jaraald was more than happy and willing to take care of Michael's sexual needs when Sarge was fulfilling his military obligations during weekdays on base. By the time Sarge was discharged Michael was through a great deal of the first phase of his transition to becoming a female. After those six months he had developed a huge set of boobs and his good sized dick had become of little importance in giving him erotic stimulation and sexual pleasure. Lenny and Jaraald spent more time with Michael during these six months than did Sarge under the circumstances, therefore Michael attached himself and bonded physically and emotionally to Lenny and Jaraald. He slept with them and they both smothered him with the comfort, love and sex that he needed. Lenny often said it was good that Jaraald was as sexually potent as he was, because he was constantly being pawed and molested by what he eventually started calling his two bitches, but always with a big smile and about 14 inches of black meat for them to share like two wanton nymphomaniacs. Fortunately Lenny was more than happy to share his hubby with Michael, so there were no bitch fights along the way. However, until Sarge was finally discharged and living full time with Michael in the big house, Michael constantly gravitated to

Jaraald, having completely bonded with the big guy with the magnificent black anaconda style super juicer. In time Sarge took Michael to Mexico for the final stage of his transition to womanhood, otherwise referred to as transsexual.

As planned, Jaraald brought Sarge, now Axel Wood in as a full partner in 'The Stables' operation. The two did convert the big Tutor house into a five star hotel and convention center. They built another ultra modern house on that view property Jaraald had wanted for years looking down on Seattle. Jaraald and Axel found it perfectly natural to continue sharing their wives with each other on a regular basis, as they had all become as one over the years. The two couples eventually adopted two biracial children each, sold the business and moved to the wonderful warm climate along the Atlantic coast in Miami, Florida.

As for Rolf and Jamie, they continued to remain a couple for a few months spending many weekends in Seattle with Axel, Michael, Jaraald and Lenny, until eventually Jamie Whiteman re-enlisted and was reassigned to the Presidio of San Francisco. Sgt. Rolf was promoted to Master Sergeant, remained in the US Army, and ended up eventually getting sent to Vietnam where he lost his life as so many others did during the Vietnam War.

ABOUT THE AUTHOR

The author was born and raised in a small community in the Sierra Foothills of Northern California where he attended elementary and high school. After completing college and a hitch in the US Army as a draftee, he worked as an accountant for a number of years. He found pushing numbers and restricted to an office environment day after day far too boring and changed careers, working as an executive officer until his retirement in 2001.

Since retirement he has moved back to the community where he was born to enjoy what some refer to as their golden years. He travels often, works in the garden, attends a cardio therapy exercise class three days a week, and spends a great deal of his time reading, writing and pounding the piano ivories.

"Virgin Army Boy Deflowered" is his first published book, after having a few short stories posted on a free web site on the Internet over a period of years since his retirement. He is working on a second alternative lifestyle novel he may possibly submit for publication in the not to distant future, depending on how well this, his first is received by you the readers.

www.ingramcontent.com/pod-product-compliance
Lightning Source LLC
Chambersburg PA
CBHW071227260626
47162CB00004B/1448